I0847499

wicked winemakers

CENTRAL COAST
FIRST LABEL
—BOOK THREE—

PRESS'
Passion

USA TODAY BESTSELLING AUTHOR
HEATHER SLADE

Table of Contents

Prologue

Luisa

"It warms my heart to see you two together. We've missed you around here," Sorcha said to Press when he and I approached her.

I waited for him to argue, tell Sorcha we weren't together, but he only thanked her for her hospitality.

"Are you stayin' here tonight, then?" she asked.

"At Seahorse. But I'll return before zero eight hundred."

"Shame," she said, nudging me with her elbow.

"Sorcha," her husband, Laird, admonished.

She rolled her eyes and winked at me before saying good night.

"I fear Sorcha is getting the wrong idea about you and me," Press said when we walked up to the door of the cottage where I was staying on Sorcha and Laird's Butler Ranch.

"She's not the only one," I mumbled more than said.

"My apologies."

"What for?"

"If people getting the wrong impression about you and me makes you uncomfortable."

"It doesn't." I leaned up, kissed his cheek, and went inside.

I'd just finished brushing my teeth, washing my face, and changing into the sweats and T-shirt I slept in when my phone vibrated. I threw myself on the bed and grabbed it, hoping it was Press, asking if I wanted him to read to me before I went to sleep, something he did to help me keep my nightmares at bay.

Instead, when I swiped the screen, I screamed.

Part I

1

"I'm tired, and I have a lot of homework to do tonight, Jorge. Please just drop me off at my mom's," I said when we left the restaurant where we'd had dinner.

"You can hang out a little while longer. We'll watch a movie. You can pick."

I didn't want to go to Jorge's tonight or any other night. I couldn't stand his roommates and wasn't too crazy about him anymore, either. I should've broken up with him before our date tonight, but as usual, I'd chickened out. It wasn't that I was afraid to do it as much as I hated confrontation. I had skirted it all my life.

My childhood memories were riddled with recollections of my parents fighting. The last was when my dad left for a bar after dinner and never came back. He didn't die that night; four other people did. A father, a mother, and their two kids were on their way home

"

when a drunk driver plowed into their car head-on, killing them all instantly. The driver, my father, survived. But, he lingered in a coma for four years. Long enough for our family to lose everything—all our money, him, and my mother, since she spent every day of those four years sitting beside his hospital bed.

That same year, I lost all my friends too, except for one. Jada Yáñez. She stuck by me no matter how horribly every other kid at our school picked on me for being a "murderer's kid." They taunted me daily, saying I should've been the one who died. And everyday, I wished I had.

The only thing that stopped me from killing myself back then was what it would have done to my sister, Seraphina. She'd already lost more than I had. Instead of being a carefree college student, she became my surrogate mom when she was eighteen and I was twelve, since she was basically all I had.

Was that when my inability to stick up for myself began, or had I always been this way? I remembered very little about my life before my father's accident.

I looked over at Jorge, wishing that when I said I wanted to go home, my *boyfriend* respected me enough to take me there. Was that on him or me?

Instead of forcing the issue, I'd do what I always did—sit through a movie I didn't want to watch, because even though Jorge said I could pick, he'd say he was sick of whatever I chose and put on one of the stupid action movies I'd endured countless times. Then, after he fell asleep, I'd call a car service to take me home since I knew he'd refuse to get up and drive me there either tonight or before my class tomorrow morning.

I'd lost count of the number of times my still-best friend Jada browbeat me for not ending things with him. Sadly, I ended up avoiding her because I didn't want to listen to it. My mom was on my ass about him too, saying she didn't trust him and didn't want me to bring him over anymore.

That was part of the reason I didn't end things with him tonight. He'd overheard her. So instead of going through with my own plan, I wound up trying to make him feel less bad about what my mother had said.

Maybe once I graduated, in a couple of months, I'd finally do what *I* wanted to do—get out of San Luis Obispo and start a new life for myself. Otherwise, I'd never dig myself out of the rut I felt I was in.

It would be hard to leave Seraphina, but I needed a break from my mom, since all she did was argue with me the same way she had with my dad.

"Your mother doesn't want you to see me anymore," said Jorge right before we pulled up to his rental house. I cringed at the look on his face. I'd seen it before on my dad's and my mom's. He was pushing for a fight. One I didn't want to have.

When I didn't respond, he reached over and pinched my nipple hard enough to hurt.

"Don't." I tried to pull his fingers away, but he grabbed my wrist with his other hand.

"You didn't answer me," he said, pinching harder.

"I told you earlier, I don't listen to her. I'm an adult." While I said the words, I sure didn't feel like one presently. "*Stop it.* That hurts," I said when he tightened his grip and twisted.

"Quit being a baby. It doesn't hurt."

"Yes, it does," I cried, reaching for the door handle.

Jorge let go of my wrist and grabbed my arm. "Okay, okay. I was just playin' with you. Don't get so mad."

"I want to go home."

"Come inside. We'll watch our movie, then I'll take you."

As mad as I was, I thought about getting out and walking home. However, I didn't feel safe in Jorge's neighborhood during the day. Nighttime was worse.

"One movie, then you'll take me home?" I bit my lip like I always did when I was uncomfortable.

"I promise."

He always promised, but never followed through.

"I'm experimenting with a new margarita recipe," he said, handing me a glass after he'd put on the action flick I predicted he would. "Let me know what you think."

I swirled the ice and liquid with the straw and took a sip.

"Do you like it?"

"It's okay. Something's off. Maybe too much alcohol."

He took it back into the kitchen. "I added a little cranberry juice. See if that helps," he said, returning and handing it to me.

Like before, I swirled the glass' contents, then took a sip. "Yeah, it's better," I said, eyeing the beer he had in his hand. "Aren't you having one?"

"Nah, I made it especially for you."

"What did you put in this?" I asked a few minutes later when my head began to throb and I had trouble focusing on the television screen.

"I told you. Cranberry—"

I felt the glass slipping out of my hand, but I couldn't get my arm to move fast enough to catch it. Then everything went black.

2

Press

Those gathered—all brothers, some by blood, some not—knew better than to speak before the man who'd called the emergency meeting of Los Caballeros arrived. The secret society dating back to our grandfathers' grandfathers only met when absolutely necessary.

"I've asked you here tonight because someone needs our help," said Noah Ridge, the last to show up. "Seraphina Reeve's younger sister, Luisa, is missing. She hasn't been seen in four days, after she left the apartment she shared with her mother, Leah."

I pulled out my tablet and made notes of everything Ridge said as he briefed the group on the details he'd learned earlier this evening from Seraphina.

Luisa was believed to have gone out with a boyfriend—Jorge, last name unknown—after an argument with her mother. Her cell phone, computer, social media, and bank accounts hadn't shown any activity since. That was enough to make the disappearance seem suspicious. However, that the missing woman was in her final weeks as a summa cum laude graduate student in Cal Poly San Luis Obispo's MBA program and hadn't attended a single class in those four days made it even more so.

When Ridge called for questions, I cleared my throat. "You said Ms. Reeve only knows her sister's boyfriend's first name."

"Correct," he responded.

"Would it be possible for us to obtain a photograph of both him and the missing sister?"

Each member of Los Caballeros brought with him a specific skill set. Mine was with technology as it related to security and intelligence. Once I had a photo, I could make several things happen.

First, I'd run the man's image through the facial recognition software I had access to. It was as powerful as the one used by the US government. Second, once I had a hit on who he was, I'd use the same software to track his movements not just in the last week, but the last several.

It was after midnight by the time Ridge adjourned our meeting. All those present had their marching orders, so to speak, for the following days.

What I discovered less than forty-eight hours later was worse than I could have imagined. Jorge, real name Manual Varilla, was a Mexican national on the FBI's wanted list for human trafficking.

Rather than contacting Ridge with the news first, I placed a call to the senior member of Los Caballeros who'd taken on more of an advisory role in recent years, Tryst Avila.

"This may be beyond our capabilities," Tryst said after I briefed him on what I'd learned. "I will see what support is available to us. Request the *caballeros* meet at Seahorse in an hour."

The place he'd referred to was my oceanfront estate just south of Cambria on the Central Coast of California. While we typically gathered in the room where we'd been two nights ago, during daylight hours, it was more difficult to do so without being detected by vineyard staff. Since I'd outfitted my house with the same level of security as the Pentagon—truthfully, mine was probably harder to penetrate—it was often our second choice.

Once everyone had arrived, Tryst spoke to the group. First, he brought those in attendance up to speed on what I'd learned about the missing woman's so-called boyfriend.

"Earlier, I was able to call in support from our friends at K19 Security Solutions," he began. The organization, a private intelligence firm, was headed up by a local man, Kade "Doc" Butler. His father, Laird, aka Burns, had developed the technology I used to identify Varilla and to secure my home.

"Through their help, we've received intel suggesting Manual Varilla and his crew of human traffickers may be operating out of the port of Yavaros in Mexico."

"That's less than two hours from your place in Alamos," said Ridge before I had the chance.

Tryst owned several thousand acres of property in the Mexican state of Sonora. A few years ago, when his wife became gravely ill, he'd made it his home full-time. He'd named the ranch *El Lugar de Curación*, or in English, the Healing Place. Sadly, his wife's health never improved and she passed away within a few months.

"You are correct," said Tryst. "I've already engaged people there to begin surveillance in advance of our and K19's arrival. They have been given authorization to immediately act if they see anyone matching Luisa Reeve's description, along with any other individuals they deem to be in danger. K19 is assembling a team. I suggest we do the same and meet them in Alamos."

I turned to my brother. "With Beau's approval, I'd like to offer the use of our plane for transport." We used the Cessna he and I owned jointly to travel back and forth from Napa Valley, where one of our family's vineyard estates was located. Seahorse's five-hundred-acre mile of shoreline served as an ideal landing strip. I'd also had a hangar built to store the plane on the property.

With the aircraft's maximum travel speed of six hundred miles per hour, we could be at Tryst's ranch in a little over ninety minutes.

"What is your recommendation as far as when we deploy?" asked Ridge, who'd requested Luisa's sister attend the meeting with him.

"As soon as possible," Tryst responded.

Ridge looked from him to me. "Would the two of you determine who should remain here and who should go to Alamos?"

"We will," I assured him.

"May I speak?" asked Seraphina.

"Of course," Ridge told her.

"First, please know I appreciate your help in finding my sister very much, so when I say this, it is solely out of concern for her."

Ridge prompted her to continue.

"Can we afford to wait? If Varilla did kidnap her, he may have already taken her out of the country, and if it was to Mexico, she might not be there any longer either."

"May I?" Tryst asked.

"Please," Ridge responded.

"I can assure you Varilla will not be leaving the port by land, water, or air."

"How—" Seraphina must've realized mid-sentence she was about to ask a question she wouldn't receive an answer to. "One more thing." She looked around the room as if to warn those present not to challenge her. "I will be on the team going to Alamos."

The only person who commented was Tryst. "As I would expect you to be," he said, looking her in the eye.

After landing the plane on the ranch's private runway, I'd just gotten settled in one of its many guesthouses, or *casitas*, when Tryst received a call requesting our support in Yavaros.

"Good God," I muttered upon our arrival at the port. There were rows and rows of warehouses, shipping containers stacked twenty deep, and ships lined up for what looked like miles, waiting to be loaded before setting off to places around the world.

"Are you certain this is where we're intended to meet?" I asked Beau when we arrived at the specified location after the sun had set.

My brother looked at something on his phone, then between two rows of stacked containers around us. "Yes, this is where Ares said to wait."

"Who is this guy connected to?" Ridge asked.

"K19, but their Shadow Ops team," Beau responded right before a man I immediately knew was Ares, based on his appearance alone, rounded the corner. The man was the Marvel graphic novel character personified.

After introducing ourselves to him, he handed out comms devices to each of us, then instructed us to stay out of the way until our assistance was needed.

Prior to our arrival, we'd been briefed on what that "assistance" entailed. First, to identify Luisa Reeve if the Shadow Ops team found where the human trafficking victims were being held. Two, to help transport the victims to a place where they could receive the necessary medical care as well as to begin the reunification process.

Tryst had stayed at the ranch in order to line up medical personnel, who would remain on standby there.

"How many men do you have going in?" Ridge asked Ares.

"Six, and from what we can tell, there may be as many as thirteen people being held in that container over there." He pointed three stacks down and one row over. "As far as what we're up against, based on thermal imaging, there's a total of sixteen inside. We believe the two people who appear to be moving about are with Varilla. Our intention is to keep the three assailants alive enough for questioning."

Alive enough. Ares' response chilled me to the bone. Like before, I felt as though those of us representing

Los Caballeros were in far over our head. We weren't trained for this or any other kind of official mission.

After making sure we were all armed, Ares took his leave.

We were able to keep track of what was happening through the comms, so we knew the precise moment the team of six made their move into the shipping container. First, we heard shouting, followed by gunshots and people screaming.

"Let her go, Varilla. The container is surrounded. There's no way out," I heard Ares shout through the earpiece.

"You let me go, or she dies," a man responded.

"If she dies, you die."

"Traer el coche," Varilla was overheard saying. I knew enough Spanish to recognize he'd just requested backup in the form of transportation through his own comms.

Within seconds, an SUV with blacked-out windows barreled up to the back of the shipping container, tires screeching.

"Four incoming," Ridge said as they jumped out of the vehicle.

"Take 'em out!" Ares responded.

Ridge, Beau, and I fired shots simultaneously, taking down three of the men who'd exited the vehicle.

"There's a fourth," said Ridge.

"I've got him," said Beau. A few seconds later, the other man fell to the ground. At the same time, more shots went off in the container.

We later learned one of the victims, a woman who was not Luisa, was killed and Manual Varilla had been captured.

3

Luisa

In my dream, I heard people moaning and screaming, but not clearly enough to decipher what they were saying. I tried to open my eyes to end the nightmare, but they seemed plastered shut. My head throbbed, and I was nauseated by the stench my brain conjured. When I tried to roll over, my arms and legs felt trapped by heavy weights.

I pried one eye open to find myself in total darkness. I didn't need to see to know my horrific nightmare wasn't a dream. I was in the bowels of hell.

4

Over the course of the next several hours, the K19 team interrogated Varilla. Neither Ridge, Beau, nor I were privy to the details. I couldn't speak for them, but I had no desire to be informed.

As Ares had predicted, thirteen victims were inside the shipping container in Yavaros, none of whom were Luisa Reeve. That particular container had been scheduled to leave the following morning. Its final destination was to be Yangshan Port in Shanghai, China.

"Varilla wants to cut a deal," said Ridge, who'd been studying something on his mobile. "He says he can tell us where Luisa is."

"That's great news," said Beau.

I, on the other hand, couldn't help but think there was more to it.

"*Fuck.* It's dependent on him providing proof of Luisa's life, which he hasn't been able to do," Ridge spat, confirming my fear. "I need to update Seraphina and her mother."

"We'll remain here, providing whatever assistance is required, if you'd like to return to Tryst's ranch," I offered.

Ridge conveyed his thanks and left a few minutes later.

"Do you think she's alive?" my brother asked once we were alone.

"I don't know what to think," I responded honestly.

Beau and I returned to the ranch the following morning and were exiting the SUV at the main residence when Tryst came outside.

"Varilla cracked," he reported. "Another shipping container owned by the same holding company as the one the team found last night is headed for the Port of Felixstowe, in the UK."

"From Yavaros?" I asked.

"No. From the Port of Altamira on Mexico's eastern coast. Varilla has also confirmed Luisa Reeve is in that container."

"When did it leave?" Beau asked.

"Five days ago," Tryst responded, looking at his mobile. "A team is convening to meet the ship when it arrives in port. Ares sent a brief with further details."

While I was exhausted to the point where I could barely keep my eyes open, rather than sleep, I went inside and logged on to my laptop to read Ares' message.

As opposed to only one container transporting victims, intel suggested there could be as many as ten. Thus, a full-scale raid was being coordinated between K19 Security Solutions, US Immigration and Customs Enforcement, the UK's National Crime Agency, and Military Intelligence Section 5—Britain's equivalent of the US Department of Homeland Security. Ares also mentioned Interpol was on standby, should further assistance be required.

The brief went on to say K19 was sending eight from their primary team and four from their second unit, Shadow Operations. They'd also requested support from the six Los Caballeros who'd participated in the raid on the single container in Yavaros. Like before, our main role would be victim assistance.

We were scheduled to leave on a flight out of Ciudad Obregón Airport this afternoon. Given the container ship's arrival time couldn't be pinpointed until the day of, we would remain on standby in London until such time as we were needed in Felixstowe.

While the K19 teams stayed in a hotel near Eaton Square, those of us from Los Caballeros stayed in a triplex my family owned in the same area.

The day after our arrival in the UK, we received word the container ship would reach the port in approximately twenty-four to thirty-six hours and the team would be deploying within an hour's time.

Once we reached Felixstowe, I was tasked with assisting the medical triage setup while K19 mapped out the raid.

When their meeting ended, Cayman, one of the Shadow Ops operatives, briefed us on what to anticipate. "Right before the ship berths, the terminal, including the vessel itself, will go entirely dark. At the same time, ear-piercing sirens will blare through the loudspeakers." He handed each of us over-ear protection. "Both of these tactics are intended to distract and confuse the traffickers guarding the victims. Thermal imaging will be used to confirm the containers to be raided. Each of them will then be liberated simultaneously. Any questions?"

My mind was reeling with them. However, none of them were need-to-know at the present time.

Before he could tell us more, Ridge burst through the back door of the warehouse where we were assembled, saying we'd been misinformed and the ship would be arriving earlier than our latest update.

"I overheard the terminal manager say he'd switched the SSA numbers, giving whoever he was talking to an extra twenty-four hours to get everything off-loaded," he said.

"If those receiving this cargo think they have twenty-four hours, it means we can anticipate the ship arriving at nightfall," said Doc in a hushed voice. "Find the damn thing," he said to Cayman before turning to those of us standing within hearing range. "Only those you trust with your *own* life get briefed on this."

"It'll be berthed in less than an hour," said Cayman, watching via overheads—or satellites—as the tugboats pulled the vessel in. It was shortly after nightfall, as Doc had predicted.

What followed could only be described as organized chaos. Assembled teams donned tactical gear, tested communications systems, and readied firearms.

As Cayman had forewarned, the entire terminal went dark and sirens began blaring. We listened via the comms as teams moved through the containers, each with a Doppler device for thermal imaging.

"Team three in place," Ares reported.

"Four in place," said Cayman.

"One in place," said Doc.

This continued until the first eight units were in position and ready to open the containers. Since the other two were mid-stack, they took longer to find. It also took additional time to move the elevated platforms where they needed to be. Once those team leaders announced they were ready, Gunner issued the command to start opening doors.

While I'd anticipated shouting and some gunfire, I picked up on neither. Instead, one by one, I heard the team leaders shouting to stand down.

"Jesus Fucking Christ," we heard Gunner say. "All clear. Get your asses over here."

The victim-assistance teams moved out one by one. Shortly after Gunner's signal, I heard several of the other teams calling out Luisa's name.

"We got her. She's in container three," said Ares right about the same time the sirens went silent and the terminal's lights came on.

"Condition?" Ridge asked through the comms as Beau and I raced out to the container beside this one.

"Stable."

My brother reached our destination first, and when Ares pointed to Luisa, he rushed forward and wrapped her in a blanket. He was leading her out when Seraphina ran up and met them at the door.

"Luisa!" she shouted.

I stood back, watching the sisters embrace.

"You take them in," Ridge instructed Beau while I followed him over to the container.

"Good God," I muttered when we reached its entrance. I covered my nose and mouth with my hand. Ridge did the same.

While I could see blankets and piles of garbage, it was the stench from waste that overpowered my senses. I rushed in when I saw a woman attempting to stand and looking as though she might pass out at any moment. With Ridge on one side and me on the other, we got her off the ship and into the triage center.

Once she was safely inside, he and I returned to assist more victims. It took two hours for us to move those rescued from the containers into the triage center and for them to be examined by the intake staff.

When there were no more victims to escort, Ridge and I walked over to where Doc sat with Ares and Kodiak, another agent on K19's team.

"Is there an arrest count?" he asked.

It occurred to me that I hadn't heard anything about the traffickers who'd been in the containers.

"Zero," said Gunner. "The fuckers locked them in. The only trap doors were epoxied shut and painted over on the inside, so there was no way for them to escape."

"How did they breathe?" Ridge asked.

"Fans hooked to car batteries circulated air from somewhere," said Ares. "Teams are processing each of the containers now."

Sickened, I couldn't listen to the rest of what was said. Instead, I walked over to where Beau and Seraphina sat with Luisa.

When I approached, she looked up, and our eyes met.

"Hello," I said, kneeling down. "I'm Press, Beau's brother."

"Hi," she said, her gaze riveted on mine.

"How are you feeling? Can I get you anything?"

"There's Ridge," Seraphina said, standing and rushing over to him.

"I'd like to sit up," Luisa said after her sister left.

I put my hand on her back as support.

"Thanks," she said, turning to bend her legs so her feet touched the floor beside the cot.

"Luisa, this is the knight in shining armor I told you about, Noah Ridge," said Seraphina, who approached with her arm through his.

Luisa shifted to get up, but Ridge knelt down and took her hand.

"Thank you," she said to him like she had to me. When her eyes filled with tears, which quickly turned into sobs, I shifted to sit beside her, but Beau got there before I did. I couldn't explain the feeling that came over me as I watched him gather her in his arms, other than to say I wished it had been me instead.

"Luisa," said Seraphina, resting her hand on her sister's knee. "Remember I told you earlier we had a place in London where we can stay until you're well enough to return home?"

Luisa nodded.

"Do you feel ready to leave now?"

She looked up at me. "You're going with us too, right?"

"I can if you'd like."

She turned to Beau. "I think I'd be more comfortable, if you don't mind coming with us."

"Let me verify we're no longer needed," I said, about to walk away.

"I'll check," offered Beau. "You'll get everyone to the SUV, yes?"

"Of course."

Luisa slipped her arm through mine. "Thank you," she said again. "My sister said we'll be staying at your place."

"Yes, we will," I responded. As we walked out to the vehicle, I told her about the triplex. "Since there are three flats in total, we'll ensure someone is with you and your sister at all times, should you need anything."

Rather than respond with words, Luisa squeezed my arm and rested her head on my shoulder.

I'd often wondered about people who said they'd lay down their life for another. I now knew exactly how they felt. I would do anything for Luisa Reeve. *Anything.*

The following day, Beau and I accompanied Luisa and her sister back to the US on a plane owned by K19. Two of their contracted pilots were in the cockpit and had been instructed to make use of our landing strip at Seahorse.

"I don't think it's safe for Luisa or her mother to return to their apartment in San Luis Obispo," I said to my brother partway through the flight.

"What are you thinking?"

"I've plenty of room at the beach."

He nodded. "I think I'll stay on as well."

While it wasn't unusual for him to do so, October was the end of crush season in the winery. In his absence, our father had overseen this year's harvest, but given he was head winemaker, I was stunned Beau wasn't anxious to return to Napa.

Perhaps, like the rest of us, he was exhausted and would head north after a couple of days' rest.

I excused myself to the aircraft lavatory, and when I returned, I overheard him mention my plan to Luisa.

"We don't want to impose," said Seraphina when I approached.

"Not at all," I said, shooting a look at my brother. "It was my idea, and I'd be happy to have you stay on as long as you're comfortable doing so." My eyes met Luisa's. "Like at the flat, I can assure you, every security measure is already in place."

"My mom…"

I sat down beside her. "It was to be a surprise, but she will be there, waiting, when we arrive. I've invited her to stay on as well."

She leaned into me and rested her head on my shoulder like she had when we were leaving Felixstowe. "I don't know how to thank you, Press."

Perhaps it was too forward of me, but I leaned down and brushed her forehead with my lips. "Your comfort and safety is all that matters."

When I raised my eyes, my brother shot me a look similar to the one he'd received from me.

5

Luisa

My mom and I were sitting on chaise lounges on Press' deck, looking out at the ocean, when my sister joined us.

"How are you doing?" she asked. "It's a little chilly right by the ocean. Can I get you another blanket?"

I smiled and pointed to the ground beside the chaise. "Beau brought out two more. Press did too."

"They're so attentive," my mother commented. "Will you be out here for a bit?" she asked Seraphina.

"Definitely," my sister responded.

"I might lie down inside, if you don't mind."

"I should probably check in with my office," Seraphina said a few minutes later.

I reached out and took her hand. "What's going on? You seem troubled about more than me."

"I don't want to go back to work," she admitted.

"Who does? Especially after being here."

"The Barrett brothers will definitely spoil you," Seraphina muttered, looking out at the ocean, her expression not one I'd expect with the words she spoke.

"What else is bothering you? I know it's more than work."

"I've been trying to reach Noah Ridge."

"He's giving us time."

"I know, but I haven't talked to him since we returned to the apartment in London. It feels wrong. Like something's up."

"Have you asked Press or Beau?" It was Press who'd said Noah was "giving us time." I didn't question it since everything after my rescue had been a whirlwind.

"Both are mum on the subject."

The door opened, and Beau joined us. "Can I get you, ladies, anything?"

"Nothing for me, thanks," said Seraphina.

I disagreed. "Actually, there is something she needs. Can you please arrange to have Noah Ridge delivered?"

"We're fresh out of Noahs, but how about some pizza?" said Beau, laughing. I chuckled too until I saw the look on my sister's face.

She and Beau went inside at the same time Press came out.

"You're probably tired of everyone asking how you are," he said, sitting on the chaise Seraphina had vacated.

"Honestly, I feel numb. I don't know what I think about anything."

"You're still in shock. It's to be expected."

"Is it?" I asked.

Press nodded. "When you feel ready, I can make arrangements for a therapist to come to Seahorse."

"What made you choose that name? Or was it already called that when you bought it?"

He smiled and looked out at the water. "It's one of the few places where it's still possible to ride horses on the beach. Sounds a bit trite when I explain it that way."

"Do you have horses?" I asked.

"I do." He pointed north. "There's a stable as well as a barn on the property."

"What's the difference?"

"A stable houses horses, whereas a barn will often be used for other livestock or to store machinery."

"You're that guy, aren't you?"

He smiled. "Which guy is that?"

"The one everyone goes to for answers."

He laughed. "I suppose I am a bit of a know-it-all."

We were quiet for a couple of minutes while I thought about his response. "I want you to know I didn't mean anything bad by what I said. I actually find it reassuring."

"That's kind of you to say."

"You don't believe me."

Press turned his head and looked into my eyes.

"Like that," I said before he had a chance to speak.

"What do you mean?"

"When you look at me like that…I'm not sure how to explain it other than to say it makes me feel like I'm going to be okay."

His eyes bored into mine. "I will do everything within my power to make sure you are, Luisa. I promise."

I'd never once believed it when Jorge promised anything, but with Press, I did. I shuddered.

"Are you cold?" he asked.

"No. I was just thinking about Jorge." I shook my head. "Seraphina said that wasn't his real name."

Press reached out and took my hand. "He is in custody and will spend the rest of his life in prison."

"I know. It's just that he used to make promises he'd never keep." I squeezed his fingers. "But you will, won't you, Press?"

"Always."

"Pizza's here. Who's hungry?" said Beau.

I hadn't been a few minutes ago when he first mentioned pizza. Now, I was, though. "I'm actually starving."

Before I realized what was happening, Beau swept me into his arms.

"What are you doing?" I said, laughing.

"We can't expect you to walk if you're *starving*, fair lady." When his gunmetal-blue eyes met mine and he smiled, I nearly gasped. Both Beau and his brother were movie-star handsome. However, Beau was more flirtatious. Press was the steady, reliable of the two.

"I'm going into the office today," my sister said the following morning when I came out of the bedroom.

I looked up at the clock and saw it was a little after nine. "When did you get up?" I asked.

"Maybe an hour ago." She seemed as preoccupied as she did yesterday.

"Why don't you just quit?"

"What a good idea." She pulled an envelope out of her bag and waved it in the air.

"What's that? A resignation letter?"

"Yep, and the sooner I get it over with, the better."

"Where are you off to?" Beau asked, joining my sister and me in the kitchen, wearing a pair of jeans but no shirt or shoes.

"To my office. I thought it best to check in." She turned to our mom, who I hadn't seen sitting in the dining room. "I'll be back soon. Um, can I borrow your car?"

Beau pulled a key fob out of his pocket and handed it to her. "Take mine. It's the red Audi."

"Um, thanks. I won't be long," she said, walking out the front door.

"Is she okay?" Beau asked.

"She has a lot on her mind," my mom responded.

"So," said Beau, turning to me just as I let my eyes trail from his ridiculously handsome face, down his ladder of abs, to the patch of hair right above the button on his jeans. "Luisa?"

While I felt almost too embarrassed to look him in the face, I did anyway. "Um, yes?"

"Press mentioned you asked if he had horses."

I nodded, feeling too stupid to speak after so openly ogling him. What made it even worse was that forty-eight hours ago I was rescued from a shipping container where I'd been held along with sixty other human trafficking victims. I shook my head and put my hand on my stomach.

"Hey," said Beau, pulling me into his arms. "What just happened?"

I turned my head when I heard footsteps, and my eyes met Press'. "I'm okay," I said to Beau, taking a step back.

"I thought maybe you'd like to go for a ride on the beach."

"Yeah, um, that sounds nice. Would you, um, excuse me?" I rushed down the hallway and into the bathroom. I would've lost the contents of my stomach, but since it was empty, all I did was dry-heave. "Go away," I groaned when I heard a knock at the door.

"Luisa, it's Mom."

"You can come in."

She knelt beside me on the floor and rubbed my back. "I wish I had a way to make it all go away, baby."

I sat back on my heels. "Nothing can make it go away, Mom."

"I know. I just—"

"Press said he could make arrangements for someone to come to Seahorse. A therapist I can talk to."

"That sounds like a very good idea, but…"

"But what?"

She waved her hand in front of her face and shook her head.

"No, tell me. But what?" I bit my lip hard enough that it hurt.

"I was going to ask if insurance covered it, but don't worry. I'll find a way to pay for it if it doesn't."

The cost hadn't even occurred to me, and she was right. Having someone come here would be far more than we could afford. "I'll look for someone my insurance covers, Mom. You don't need to worry about it."

"I'm sorry, baby."

I stood, washed my face, and brushed my teeth. "Thanks for bringing my stuff here," I said as my mom walked out of the bathroom. God, the last thing I meant to do was make her feel bad.

When I returned to the kitchen, Press was eating breakfast. Neither Beau nor my mom was with him. He stood as soon as he saw me walk in.

"Please, don't get up on my account."

He came around the island and took my hand. "What happened a few minutes ago?"

"Thinking," I got out before my eyes filled with tears.

Press dropped my hand but embraced me. As I cried, he stroked my hair.

"I'm sorry," I said, pulling back and wiping my nose with the back of my hand.

"First, do not feel as though you need to apologize to me for anything, let alone crying." He handed me a handkerchief, and I wiped my face and nose. "Second, remember what I said yesterday? As soon as you feel ready, I'll make arrangements for Dr. Benedict to come to Seahorse."

I shook my head. "I can find someone. I'll just check with my insurance."

Press rested both hands on my shoulders. "I'm going to be very frank with you. Will that be all right?"

I hated that it sounded like he was about to scold me. However, the man had invited me to stay here. If he had something to say, the least I could do was listen. "Of course."

Press put his finger on my chin. "Stop biting your lip, pet."

I glared at him, and he smiled, but it left quickly, and his tone returned to serious. "As long as you are here, which I hope will be long enough for you to heal from all you've experienced, I do not want you to worry about things like insurance."

I folded my arms. "I have no choice but to think about things like insurance, Press. I can't afford to pay a therapist to make house calls." My eyes opened wide, and I took a step back.

"What just happened?" he asked with eyes as wide as mine.

"It's going to sound stupid."

"What is?"

"It's just...I don't..."

He took a step forward. "Please, I beg you. Tell me what's happened?"

"I don't usually get so, um, feisty."

Press smiled. "Well done, then."

"Don't make fun of me."

When he reached up and caressed my cheek, I stopped biting my lip without him needing to say anything.

"I would never poke fun at you. I was completely sincere in my praise."

I squared my shoulders and took a deep breath. "I can't afford a therapist that isn't covered by my insurance."

"Please be seated." He pulled out a stool on the other side of the counter and motioned for me to sit down. "I know this isn't easy for you, and I respect everything you've said." He sat beside me. "My sole concern is that you're able to heal. And again, I know this is not easy for you to accept, but money is not an issue for me, Luisa. Please, let me do this for you."

I teared up again and dabbed my eyes with his handkerchief. "Why?"

"I made you a promise to do everything in my power to make sure you would be okay, yes?"

"Yes."

"Then, allow me to keep that promise. For now, just let me take care of the things you need. And someday in the future, if I need your help, I've no doubt you will do the same for me."

"I will."

Press smiled and tilted his head to look into my eyes. "Promise?"

"I promise."

"May I contact Dr. Benedict?" he asked.

"Yes, please."

"Hey," said Beau, joining me in the kitchen after Press left to make the call. "Everything okay?"

"It is now," I said.

"Excellent. Does this mean you're up for a ride on the beach?"

"I may have an appointment with a therapist today, but either before or after, I'd love to."

"Love to what?" Press asked, returning to the kitchen.

"Luisa and I are throwing a leg over later." Beau winked at me.

"Are you, now?" Press asked, looking at me.

"If that means riding horses on the beach, then, yes. I did tell him I might have an appointment, though."

"And you do. Dr. Benedict will be here at three this afternoon. Will that work?"

"Perfectly," Beau responded before I could. "We'll ride, followed by a picnic."

"Is that okay?" I asked Press.

"You do not need to ask my permission, pet."

I scowled. "Pet?" It was the second time he'd called me that.

"My apologies. A term of endearment I get the impression you don't care for."

"Not even a little."

"Noted. Now, if you're off to ride, I think I'll finish my breakfast and get some work done."

Beau took my hand and was leading me out the door, jabbering away about Press' horses.

"Hang on a sec," I said, dropping his hand and returning to the kitchen. "Thank you, Press. For everything."

"Not at all, Luisa."

6

Press

Over the course of the next week, Luisa met with Dr. Benedict each morning, then spent the afternoon basking in my brother's attention while I worked.

My job was to manage the assets of Barrett Family Enterprises, and fortunately, I could do it from most anywhere I had access to the internet.

Our holdings included the vineyard estates and wineries in both Northern California and here, on the Central Coast, as well as in the Burgundy region of France. Our other agricultural properties were in Norfolk and Suffolk in the northern part of East Anglia, and Cambridgeshire and Essex in the south. The family also owned commercial property throughout the United States, primarily on the east and west coasts, and in the UK, mainly in London.

My duties didn't end there, however. With the help of a staff, I managed a myriad of other investments on behalf of not just my immediate family, but for the entirety of the Barrett clan.

"Hello, pet," I said when Luisa came in after she and Beau returned from the weekly farmer's market in Cambria. "My apologies, Luisa," I added when she frowned at me.

"I thought I'd make dinner tonight, if you wouldn't mind."

"Mind? Not in the least. In fact, I'd bow down in appreciation. I haven't eaten all day."

Her eyes opened wide. "Why not?"

"Distracted by work," I said, motioning to the laptop sitting in front of me.

"Do you have to work tonight?"

I closed my computer. "Definitely not. I've already spent far too much time today doing so. What did you have in mind?"

"The second episode of the historical romance series we watched the other evening airs at seven."

"Ah, yes. The story of the duke and diamond of the first water."

"You wouldn't mind?"

"Not at all. I enjoyed it."

She raised a brow and folded her arms.

"What?"

"You *enjoyed* it?"

I chuckled. "Very much so, not that you need to broadcast that fact to anyone."

Luisa smiled. "Your secret is safe with me. I'll let you know when dinner is ready."

"Where's Beau?" I asked, realizing he hadn't come in. Not that I minded. In fact, having Luisa to myself for the evening was a dream come true.

"He said he needed to help Ridge with something."

"Excellent," I said under my breath when Luisa was out of hearing range.

An hour later, my stomach rumbled as heavenly aromas wafted from my kitchen. It was all I could do to stay put and not ask when dinner might be ready. Instead, I went outside to watch the sunset.

Luisa joined me a few minutes later.

"What's this?" I asked when she handed me a glass of wine before sitting on the chaise beside mine.

"Barrett Family Vintners Sauvignon Gris."

"Outstanding. One of my favorites," I said, swirling my glass and breathing in the bright fruit aromatics.

She set her glass on the table between us and went back inside.

"May I assist?" I called after her.

"Nope. I'll just be a minute."

This time when she returned, she brought two plates with her. "I thought we could have our appetizer out here and watch the sun go down." She handed one plate to me. "Mexican street corn flatbread with an avocado and cilantro oil drizzle. I hope you like it."

"I love it."

Luisa giggled. "You haven't tried it yet."

"I still love it."

She smiled and took a sip of wine. "You're way too nice to me, Press."

"You make it easy, pet…err …Luisa."

She rolled her eyes and took a bite of the flatbread at the same time I did.

"Well?" she asked, biting her lip as I savored the flavors of corn slathered with sour cream, Cotija cheese, lime juice, and chile on top of the crunchy crust.

"Brilliant. Truly," I said before taking another bite. "Now, stop chewing on your lip. Eat this fabulous food instead."

Luisa scowled at my correction, then beamed.

Once the sun dipped below the horizon, we went inside, where I saw the table was set for two. "Where are your mum and sister this evening?" I asked.

"My mom ate earlier and is reading, and I'm not sure about Seraphina."

"May I assist?" I repeated when she ducked into the kitchen.

"Have a seat. I'll be right out."

Like before, she carried two plates into the dining room. "You were supposed to take a seat," she said, tsking at me.

"This smells fantastic," I said when she set a plate of stuffed poblano peppers in front of me.

"The peppers are stuffed with burrata, black-eyed peas, and chorizo, then topped with pico de gallo Be right back," she said, disappearing into the kitchen again.

She returned with two bottles of Mexican beer. "I hope you don't mind. The dish doesn't pair well with any of the wine I could find."

"This is perfect." I took a bite and groaned. "You have been holding out on me. Again, this is brilliant. Where did you learn to cook like this? Your mum?"

Luisa laughed. "No. Definitely not my mom. My friend Jada's mother taught her and me to cook."

"Mrs. Yáñez?"

"Yes. She's a fantastic cook. As is Mrs. Avila. You know they're twins, right? Well, of course you do. Brix Avila is one of your best friends, isn't he?"

"Yes, one of my very best. Do you know Brix well?" I asked between bites of the luscious food she'd prepared.

"Not at all. He's quite a bit older than Jada and me."

I nearly cringed, but stopped myself. Quite a bit older and the same age as me.

"Oh, our show starts in ten minutes. Do you mind if we watch it while we have our third course?"

"I wouldn't mind at all." I'd recorded it so we didn't have to. However, Luisa was more animated tonight than I'd seen her. I would do nothing to put a damper on how much she was enjoying herself.

"I'll meet you in the living room," she said, taking our dishes into the kitchen.

I'd queued the program and taken a seat when my phone vibrated. I glanced at it, hoping it was something I could either ignore entirely or respond to later, when I saw I'd received a message from my brother.

Look who's in town, read the text. I cringed when I saw the accompanying photo of my brother and the woman who'd been his on-and-off girlfriend for years despite the fact she lived in Australia—Daphne Cullen. Something told me her presence was not going to go over well with Luisa.

I'd just turned off the television and was about to dish bowls of ice cream for Luisa and me when Beau came inside.

"You're up. Wonderful. There's someone I want you to meet," he said to Luisa.

"Hello, Press," said Daphne, kissing my cheek.

Beau grabbed her hand and pulled her away from me. "Luisa, this is Daphne. Daph, Luisa."

"It's nice to meet you," said Daphne, taking Luisa's hand in hers. "Beau has told me so much about you."

Luisa's eyes darted between Beau's, mine, and the woman's who still held her hand. "He hasn't told me a thing about you," she mumbled, biting her damn lip. God, I wanted to throttle my brother.

Daphne laughed and punched Beau's arm. "Not a thing, you say? Not a single word about the love of your life?" While she was joking, what she'd said wasn't that far off the mark, and it was evident Luisa picked up on it.

"Um, if you'll excuse me, I'm pretty tired. Good night."

I could see her tears as she hurried to the bedroom she shared with Seraphina, wishing I could follow without making more of a scene.

"Did I say something wrong?" Daphne asked.

"Of course you didn't," said Beau, leading her in the opposite direction to where his room was. "Let's get you settled."

"You're a bloody idiot," I seethed under my breath as he walked by. The look he gave me confirmed my words were right on the mark. My brother had absolutely no idea of the ramifications of what he'd done.

Rather than go to Luisa's room, I knocked on her mother's door.

"What's wrong?" she asked, opening it a crack.

"Luisa may need you."

Thankfully, she didn't ask why before hurrying across the hall and into her daughter's bedroom.

The following morning, despite my wishing it were otherwise, Luisa and her mother left Seahorse and went to stay thirty miles inland at the home of Laird and Sorcha Butler.

7

Press

Luisa spent eleven days with me at Seahorse, and now that she was gone, my house felt painfully quiet, painfully joyless.

Yes, she'd been recovering from being kidnapped and subsequently spending a week locked in a shipping container, facing horrors previously unimaginable to her. She'd struggled with self-doubt, as if she were somehow to blame for her own abduction; nightmares plagued her every night; and during the day, panic attacks came out of seemingly nowhere.

However, mixed in with the bad days, there had been good ones. Through it all, Luisa's bravery amazed me. While the therapist I'd engaged to assist with her recovery shared little to nothing with me, what she did say was that Luisa's progress astounded even her.

I recognized I was feeling pathetically sorry for myself, but I couldn't help it. I ached with missing her, and each time I closed my eyes and saw her smiling face gazing back at me, I wanted to throttle my insensitive brother.

"Good morning," Luisa said when she answered my daily call.

"Good morning to you. How's the weather inland?" It was the way we began each of our first conversations of the day for the last eight—since she'd left Seahorse.

"Sunny and beautiful. What's it like at the beach?"

"Cloudy, overcast, and downright miserable," I said. However, the misery resided more within me than with the weather. "What do you feel like doing today?"

"Jada is coming over for breakfast, then Dr. Benedict."

"I see. I suppose, then, I should attempt to get some work done."

"Can you visit this afternoon?"

"It would be my pleasure. Don't forget another episode of our duke and his diamond airs this evening. Shall I bring dinner along with me?"

"Sorcha will not be happy if you do. As for me, I'd gladly skip a meal."

"She'd notice and feed you twice as much tomorrow," I teased.

"You're right. It's her life's ambition to make me fat."

"It eases the pain of missing you, knowing she and Laird are taking such good care of you."

"I doubt you miss me, Press. You see me every day. If you were honest, you'd admit you're getting sick of me."

"I never would. Even after a lifetime of daily visits."

Even without being able to see her, I knew her cheeks were flushed and she was smiling.

I braced myself for the question that would inevitably come, wishing she would stop asking.

"Um, how's Beau? Are he and Daphne still at Seahorse?"

"They are not. They left this morning for Napa."

"Oh…Well, you must be glad to have the place to yourself."

"Not at all. In fact, if you wanted to come back—"

"Hang on, I think Jada just pulled in."

"You go ahead and greet her. I'll see you this afternoon."

"Thanks, Press," she said right before I heard the chimes of the call ending.

8

Luisa

"Were you talking to Press?" Jada asked when I opened the front door of the cottage where my mom and I had spent the last few nights.

I nodded. "He's coming over later. After I meet with Dr. Benedict."

"And Beau?"

I sighed, closing the door behind her when she came inside. "Press said he's on his way to Napa."

"And the girlfriend?"

"Going with him," I practically spat.

"He's a player. You know this," she said like she did every single time the man's name was mentioned.

"That will be Sorcha with breakfast," I said when there was another knock at the door.

"There's my two favorite lasses," she said when I invited her in. She and I cheek-kissed, then she did the same with Jada. "My Ainsley called this morning. She's hoping to pay a visit later in the week."

There'd been a time when Ainsley Butler, Jada, and I considered ourselves the three musketeers. We rarely saw her after she left for Stanford to complete her undergrad degree before getting her master's, just like I had at Cal Poly San Luis Obispo. Except I hadn't finished. It would take me less than a month to do so, and while Press encouraged me to consider going back, I couldn't bring myself to.

It was another topic of conversation Dr. Benedict and I covered regularly, along with talking about my abduction, Beau, and Press. In fact, our discussions about Press seemed to go on longer than the others.

While she hadn't come right out and said it, I knew by the way she asked that she thought I was too dependent on him. "Do you have plans to see Press today?" she'd ask. I didn't know why she bothered; the answer was always the same. Of course I had plans to see him. He visited me at Butler Ranch every day.

"What's that look for?" Jada asked.

"Thinking about my conversation with my therapist."

"I may be wrong, but dreading talking to Dr. Benedict doesn't sound conducive to beneficial therapy."

"She thinks I should 'wean' myself from Press."

Jada laughed. "I think it's the other way around, girlfriend."

"He's a nice man who cares about me. It's me who she thinks is too dependent on him." I caught a look that passed between Jada and Sorcha. "What?" I asked.

"He's a nice man who cares about you," Jada repeated my words back to me.

"Yes, that's what I said."

She rolled her eyes.

"You don't understand."

"I think it's you who doesn't understand," said Jada. "Right, Sorcha?"

While she didn't speak, Sorcha's brow was raised.

"What?" I repeated, this time directly to her.

"'Tis up to you and Press to figure out what's between you, lass. Not Jada, not me, and not Dr. Benedict."

"There's nothing to figure out. We're friends."

This time when Sorcha raised a brow, I didn't ask why.

The following morning when Press called, he asked if he could come by early in the day rather than in the afternoon.

"Of course," I told him. "You can join my mom and me for breakfast."

He arrived thirty minutes later, which meant he had to have left Seahorse the minute our call ended.

"Is everything okay?" I asked when I opened the door and invited him inside.

"Yes, fine," he responded, but I could tell it wasn't.

"Wait," I said when he walked in the direction of the kitchen. "Whatever it is, tell me."

I had panic attacks less frequently, but one of my triggers was when I thought someone was keeping something from me. I closed my eyes and practiced the breathing techniques Dr. Benedict had taught me. Press rushed over and led me to the sofa. He sat beside me and rubbed my back as I took deep breaths.

"I'm sorry, pet. It's my parents. My mum, actually. She's summoned me to Napa for a visit."

I hated it when he called me pet, but he probably didn't realize he'd done it. Usually, he caught himself and apologized.

"How long will you be gone?" I asked.

"I'm not certain. Perhaps a few days."

Dr. Benedict's concern about my dependence on him came to the forefront of my mind. The idea he'd be gone one day, let alone several, made the panic worse. It wasn't fair to him, and I knew it. I just didn't know how to make it stop.

"Talk to me, Luisa," he said, leaning forward to kiss my forehead like he did so often.

"I'll be okay. You need to see your parents." I repeated the words in my head. *I'd be fine. He had a life that didn't revolve around me. I'd be fine.*

"How's this? I'll go for the day, then return in the morning. You'll hardly know I'm gone."

"You don't have to do that, Press. I'll be—"

"Fine. Yes, I know. However, I will not be. As I spoke the words 'several days," I realized I could not possibly stay away that long."

"Press—"

"It's settled. I'll return in the morning. Now, we have some other things to talk about today, do we not?"

Over dinner last night, he'd brought up the subject of me completing my degree, like he had a couple of times before.

"Graduating."

He smiled. "I do strongly believe your professors will allow you to complete the last few assignments and exams independently, given the reason you were unable to at the end of the semester."

"Do you really think they'd let me?"

"I do."

The emphatic way he said it led me to believe he didn't "think" they would. He knew they would.

"You've talked to them, haven't you?"

Press didn't get embarrassed easily, and when he did, it was hard to catch unless someone spent as much time with him as I did. "Not with them, no. However, my father and the dean of the business school are quite good friends…My apologies if I've overstepped."

"You haven't." It wasn't just seeing him every day; I depended on Press for so much more. The man did everything he could for me, and then some. "Thank you."

"Whatever I can do to help, say the word."

I smiled.

"Next subject."

"The ranch."

Press nodded. "Have you given any further thought to visiting?"

When he told me about it last night, he'd used the word "magical." He'd also said Tryst, who was Brix's uncle—at least I thought that was what he'd said—had named the ranch *El Lugar de Curación*, which translated to the Healing Place.

"I talked to my mom about it after you left. She agreed that, even though I was missing then and she was terrified, being there somehow soothed her. She said something about it having a 'harmonious energy field' that made her feel like you were going to find me and I'd be okay."

Press nodded again. "I have experienced an inexplicable sense of peace and tranquility with every visit."

"It sounds intriguing."

"If you find yourself compelled over intrigued, say the word, and we'll visit."

We'd just finished breakfast when my phone chimed with a message from my sister.

"Everything okay?" Press asked after I'd read it.

"Seraphina and Ridge are on their way here. She said there's something important she wants to talk to me about."

"My apologies for needing to leave before they arrive, but if I intend to return tomorrow, I should be on my way."

"Don't apologize. I'll be okay," I said to myself as much as to him.

He stood, then leaned down to kiss my forehead like he always did. "Stop biting your lip, Luisa."

I did and smiled as I watched him walk away. I missed him already, something I could not admit to Dr. Benedict.

My sister was glowing when she and Ridge pulled up in front of the cottage where my mom and I sat, enjoying the sunshine.

"Hey," she said, getting out of the car and walking over to kiss my cheek. "Where's Press?"

"He had to go. Something about spending time with his mother. He may have said he was summoned."

"Speaking of being summoned, I'm supposed to help Sorcha and Bradley with tonight's dinner," said our mom. She stood and kissed Seraphina's cheek before walking away.

"I should probably go check in with my parents," said Noah, who'd walked up behind my sister.

I looked up at him. "Before you do, there's something I want to talk to you both about."

"Go ahead," said my sister when Noah pulled a chair over to sit.

I told them what Press and I had talked about last night and this morning. First, about finishing my degree, then about visiting the ranch.

"That's where we stayed when we were first looking for you," she said, squeezing my hand.

"Press also said it's *magical*. Mom agreed."

Seraphina smiled. "She did?"

"Press said he could take us there in his plane if we wanted to go."

"Press has been a busy guy," Noah said under his breath.

"I want to go, and I know you'll have a fit unless you go too. Then, when we get back, I'll finish out my classes," I said, hoping she'd agree.

"Have you brought this up to Mom?"

"I asked her about the ranch, but not about visiting. I figured you'd be the harder one to convince."

When Noah laughed, my sister smacked him. "Hush, you," she said.

My phone vibrated, and when I checked the screen, I saw it was Press calling. "Be right back," I said to my sister before going inside. "Hi," I answered.

"Change of plans, pet, I mean Luisa."

"Will you need to stay on longer?"

"Actually, I won't be going at all. My dad and I got our wires crossed, as they say. The two are leaving town as we speak."

I was about to ask where they were going, but thought better of it. My instincts told me it had something to do with Beau, and since as far as I knew, Daphne was still with him, I'd rather not know.

"I was thinking of coming back, unless you're weary of my company."

"Never."

"See you soon, Luisa."

When I came out the front door, I heard Ridge say, "You wanna know what I think?"

"I do," my sister responded.

"I think it would be the perfect place for a wedding."

"*A wedding?*" I shrieked.

"Noah proposed and I accepted," she said, smiling from ear to ear.

My eyes filled with tears, and I hugged her. "I'm so happy for you." I looked up at my future brother-in-law. "You too, Ridge. You're a lucky man."

Like Seraphina, he beamed.

A pang of envy shot through me. Would anyone ever love me the way Ridge loved my sister? I shook my head. Now wasn't the time for self-pity.

"So, where would be a perfect place for a wedding?"

"Tryst's ranch," answered Ridge.

I clapped my hands. "That's wonderful! When?"

My sister looked up at Ridge, who shrugged.

"What about Christmas?" I asked.

They both smiled and nodded. "Sounds perfect."

Part II

9

I shifted slightly and peeked at the other side of the altar at Luisa. She was the most beautiful creature God had been so kind to grace the rest of us lowly beings with. We both stood, bearing witness to the union between her sister, Seraphina, and Noah Ridge, a man who was as much a brother to me as a friend. I wasn't the best man—a position reserved for Ridge's closest mate, Brix—but I was the first groomsman. Thus, allowing me to look at the maid of honor unnoticed.

Even after all she'd been through, instead of appearing as an injured party, she wore her bravery like a badge. I couldn't be prouder of her.

In the days Luisa stayed with me at Seahorse, I'd witnessed her transformation from a victim to a survivor and, with it, had a front-row seat to the wonder of the woman. She was extraordinarily intelligent, her beauty had no equal even among the world's most recognizable supermodels, and her heart, well, it was soft and kind, gentle and loving. The evil bastards who had taken her and transported her across the ocean didn't break the spirit of the woman who stood behind her sister, tear-filled eyes smiling.

To say I loved Luisa would be unimaginable to some, yet I did with all my being. When she raised her head and gazed in my direction, my heart first leaped, then fell when she looked beyond me to my brother, who stood behind me. He was the man she was in love with rather than me, despite his cavalier and insensitive attitude when he'd paraded his longtime girlfriend in front of her.

While I was older than Beau by three years, in maturity, that number doubled—at least. It wasn't entirely his fault. As the oldest, I'd embraced every responsibility my parents asked me to. And many they hadn't. Most people who knew both him and me guessed at least a decade separated us. Where he was the life of the party, I was the one in the background, orchestrating food and drink, and making sure our guests enjoyed themselves regardless of the type of event being thrown.

I raised my head again, realizing I should be paying attention to the wedding ceremony rather than getting lost in thought over my brother and Luisa, as I so often did.

As much as I knew it would hurt, I let my eyes drift to her again, stunned when it appeared she was looking at me rather than Beau. Just to be sure, I winked. When Luisa smiled, I did too.

While she and Seraphina shared the same long dark hair, the woman whose eyes I couldn't stop myself from staring into was fairer. Rather than dark brown, her peepers—as my grandmum used to call them— were midnight black, and her complexion was more peaches-and-cream than her sister's olive-toned skin.

The red gown she wore enhanced her beauty, if that were possible, as did the pink on her cheeks after spending the last two days in the sun.

Temperatures in Alamos, Mexico, the town where Tryst Avila's *El Lugar de Curación* ranch was located and where Ridge and Seraphina's wedding was being held, averaged thirty degrees Celsius—or in the eighties Fahrenheit—in December. As opposed to Cambria, California, the place where I lived the majority of the time and where today the high would be twenty degrees cooler.

Lost in thought, my gaze traveled down the length of Luisa's body. She was a sprite of a thing, thin and athletic, yet her ample breasts strained against the bodice of her gown.

When my eyes returned to hers after my perusal, she raised a brow. Caught, I grinned and shrugged one shoulder. When she winked at me like I had, my cock stirred. A very inopportune moment for it to do so, given I was standing in full view of everyone gathered in the tiny chapel. When my brain conjured how she'd looked in the bikini she wore yesterday when we sat by the pool—tight abs, long shapely legs, and stiff nipples when the sun went behind a cloud—I angled my body farther right, toward the altar.

Moments later, when Tryst proclaimed Seraphina and Ridge "partners in the vast and wondrous universe" and suggested they kiss, I was flooded with happiness.

There'd been a time I doubted Ridge would ever marry. In the years I'd known him, he'd pined for Alex Avila-Butler, a woman in love with and married to another.

Prior to the start of the ceremony, Alex had accompanied Ridge down the aisle in a symbolic gesture of delivering him to the place where his heart would be given to Seraphina.

I shuddered and rolled my eyes. Since when was I so bloody sappy? Perhaps I should forgo my plan to remain in Alamos until after New Year's Day, and return to Cambria—given watching Luisa with Beau would break my heart into smaller bits than it already was.

Or maybe I should visit Napa Valley, where my brother and I were in the doghouse with our mum for not spending Christmas or Boxing Day with her and our father.

The last I'd seen either of my parents was in October at the Wicked Winemakers' Ball. Beau and I had agreed to participate in the night's biggest fundraiser, the bachelor auction. The same woman had bid and won dates with both of us—our mother. When Alex Avila-Butler, the fundraiser's organizer, asked why she'd done it, our mum informed her it was the only way she might have a moment's time with her two sons.

I remained contrite about my mother's motives when she did it, and still did now. However, it was later that same night that Ridge called an emergency meeting of Los Caballeros, enlisting us to find Luisa, who Seraphina had reported missing. It was what Los Caballeros did. When someone needed our help, we provided it any way we could.

I'd planned to visit my mum and dad two months ago, but I'd misunderstood their travel schedule and canceled my trip when I discovered they wouldn't be in Napa.

As the guilt I felt over not seeing them since the auction night grew, it occurred to me that if I left later today or even in the morning, I would be able to join them as they delivered toys and gifts to every shelter within a fifty-mile radius of our family's vineyard estate.

My mother and father were American—as Beau and I were—yet we had spent the majority of my childhood living in London and, thus, had celebrated many UK traditions.

December twenty-sixth was now known to most as a day for shopping. Originally, though, it was the day the aristocracy delivered "Christmas boxes" to those less fortunate. Until we were in our mid-twenties, our mum, who championed a number of charities, had insisted my brother and I accompany her and our father on their Boxing Day excursions.

I felt Beau nudge me and realized Luisa and Brix were almost to the rear of the chapel and I'd been holding up the recession of the wedding party. There weren't any more attendants on Seraphina's side, so I walked alone.

"Everything okay?" Beau asked when he followed me outside the chapel, where the bride, groom, Luisa, and Brix stood.

"Fine, fine. Just a tad nostalgic. Times are certainly changing. Two of the ten of us are now married."

I was lying; however, I could hardly tell my own brother I couldn't bear to watch Luisa pine over him. For the last several weeks, I'd had her undivided attention while Beau hosted Daphne, his childhood sweetheart who'd eventually become his on-and-off girlfriend. My guess was they were currently off since he hadn't brought her to the wedding.

Vaile "Zin" Oliver, the man I considered my best mate, joined us. "You appear more melancholy," he commented.

"Not at all. I couldn't be happier for Ridge and Seraphina." I wasn't mustering enough enthusiasm to convince myself I meant my words, let alone Beau or Zin. I lowered my voice. "The truth is I'm feeling quite guilty for being away from our parents. I'm thinking of leaving shortly after the festivities."

"Leaving to go where?" asked Luisa, who I hadn't realized was standing behind me.

"Home, actually. Or rather to my parents' home."

"In London?"

"They live in Napa," Beau answered before I had the chance.

"What he said," I muttered, excusing myself to congratulate the bride and groom.

"Press?"

"Yes," I said over my shoulder, wondering why she was following me rather than hanging on my brother's every syllable.

"Can you please stop?"

A few more paces, and I would've been close enough to give my regards to the newly married couple. Instead, I turned around. "Yes?" I repeated.

"You didn't mention you were leaving when we spoke earlier."

"Right. During the ceremony, it occurred to me I was missing one of my mum's favorite traditions."

"What?" Was I imagining the look of panic in her eyes? Luisa had no reason to worry. She would be well protected here on the ranch. I took a step closer, intending to reassure her, but once again, my brother interrupted.

"Boxing Day," he responded.

Luisa looked from Beau to me. "That's one of your mother's favorite traditions?"

"Perhaps you can explain why," I said, clapping my brother on the back. "If you remember."

I turned on my heel without looking him or Luisa in the eye. Yes, I was irritated, and I had no intention of confessing why.

"Press and Zin," said Seraphina, embracing me first, then him.

"Best wishes to you," I said. "You look stunning, by the way." I turned to Ridge, and we also embraced. "You're a very lucky man, my friend. Yours is truly a 'love match,' to quote the historical romance series that seems to be all the rage."

Seraphina put her hand on my arm. "You were kind to indulge my sister by watching every episode with her. I doubt most men would have." She laughed. "Or women."

I chuckled, wondering what she'd think if I told her we'd also started reading books together by the same author whose works had inspired the series.

My eyes met Zin's, and he smirked. He'd given me quite a ribbing for it when he arrived one evening to find Luisa and me enthralled in the series. It hadn't been all bad. I had to admit I enjoyed watching Luisa's reactions to the sex scenes that were far more graphic than I'd anticipated. At first, I'd been concerned they might trigger an unpleasant memory. However, they had the opposite effect on her. It appeared to turn her on as much as it did me. *Not* something I could think about at the moment, though.

"As I was saying, congratulations, Ridge. I envy you." I hadn't intended to say the last bit aloud, but there it was. The words hung heavy in our mutual silence.

"Thanks, Press." He squeezed my shoulder, no doubt correctly assuming my comment related to Luisa.

I cleared my throat. "I wanted to let you know I'll be leaving in the morning to spend the day with my parents."

"I'm sorry we took you away from them on Christmas." Seraphina's eyes were downcast.

I shook my head. "You were kind enough to ask prior to scheduling the wedding. I'm sure I speak for everyone here when I say there isn't anywhere we'd rather be."

"I'm glad you're sticking around to celebrate with us, at least," said Ridge.

"Speaking of which, let's get this party started," said Zin.

He and I were on our way into the tent where the festivities would take place when I heard someone shout my name. Not "Press," as everyone called me, but Lavery, my given first name. I clasped my hands behind my back and slowly turned around. When my gaze settled on Luisa, I raised a brow.

She stalked toward me, wearing heels and attempting to stomp her feet on the grass. Once within a foot of me, she folded her arms. "Why are you avoiding me?"

I grinned. "I'm hardly avoiding you, pet."

She bristled at the term of endearment she'd told me more than once she didn't care for. However, I was in no mood to indulge her.

"When will you be back?" she asked in a voice far less accusatory than it had been with her last question. The other tell of her distress was that she was biting her lip.

"Back? If you mean when will I return to Tryst's ranch, I don't intend to do so. At least not in the immediate future."

"But…"

"If you have a question, ask it." For the second time, I did nothing to mask my irritation—until her eyes filled with tears. Then I drew her into my arms like I had so many times in the last few weeks, comforting her as I would a sister instead of the woman I longed to make mine. "Tell me why you're crying."

"I'm not," she said, wriggling out of my arms. "You're the one—"

"I'm not crying, either." I smiled.

Luisa huffed but didn't walk away. "I'm wondering why you didn't mention you were leaving."

"I hadn't decided until a few minutes ago. If you're concerned about staying on here without me, you needn't be. You are not my guest; you are Tryst's." I'd spent enough time with Luisa to be familiar with many of her expressions. She had something else she wished to ask. "Whatever it is, just say it, pet."

"Don't call me that."

"Very well. Whatever it is, just say it, Luisa."

"Never mind."

When she stalked away, I didn't follow. I'd spent the last two months repeatedly inserting myself in her life in any way she'd have me. Thus, she'd become dependent on me, and that wasn't healthy for either of us.

10

Luisa

I glanced over my shoulder. Rather than follow me into the tent where the wedding celebration would be taking place, Press went in the opposite direction.

"What's wrong?" Seraphina met me at the tent's entrance.

"Press is leaving," I said, biting my lower lip.

She took both my hands in hers. "Not until tomorrow." My sister cocked her head. "Luisa..."

I rolled my shoulders and forced a smile. "I was surprised, that's all." When a man walked past us with a tray of champagne, I grabbed two glasses and handed one to her. "I'm so happy for you," I said, raising mine in a toast. She touched my glass with hers, and I took a sip.

"Come with me," she said, tucking my arm in hers and leading me over to where Ridge was talking to Brix and Beau.

"I hope you'll save me a dance," said Beau, the man whose very presence made my pulse race even though I knew he wasn't the slightest bit interested in me.

"I suppose, as the only bridesmaid, I'll need to save a dance for all the groomsmen."

Rather than respond, Beau pulled his phone out and studied the screen. "Where's Press?" he asked abruptly, looking between Ridge and Brix.

"Not sure. Why?" Ridge asked.

"I need to speak with him." Beau excused himself and left the tent.

"I'll find out what's happening," offered Brix when Ridge appeared he might follow.

Did it make me a narcissist to wonder if whatever they needed to talk about had something to do with me? Or was it normal, given it had only been two months since my abduction?

Due to the holidays, as well as my sister's wedding, it had been over a week since I last spoke with my therapist. We didn't have another appointment sched-uled until after the first of the year. She'd said that if I felt as though I needed to talk sooner, I could send a message, and she'd make the arrangements. I wouldn't do so today, but maybe tomorrow. Especially since

Press announcing he was leaving filled me with dread. Foreboding might be a better word. Panic fit too.

My dependence on him was a regular topic of conversation between Dr. Benedict and me. As was the crush I had on Beau. The latter didn't seem to concern her quite as much as the former. While she hadn't suggested I go "cold turkey," as they say, she had advised I begin weaning myself from Press.

I wasn't as worried about him saying he was leaving tomorrow and had no plans to return to Tryst's ranch as I was that he hadn't mentioned when we might see each other again, if ever.

I'd gone from staying with him at Seahorse to doing the same at Butler Ranch. Was it time for me to return to the apartment my mom and I shared in San Luis Obispo?

I gripped the back of a nearby chair when I felt a full-blown panic attack coming on just from thinking about living there again. It wasn't as though Jorge—Manual Varilla, as I had to repeatedly remind myself—had taken me from the apartment. The last thing I remembered before waking up bound and gagged in a shipping container was going to his place after we'd had dinner together.

"Luisa?" My sister covered my hand with hers. "Why don't we sit down for a few minutes?"

"I'm okay," I said, focusing on the breathing exercises Dr. Benedict had taught me to calm myself when I felt an imminent attack.

"Sit with me anyway." Seraphina led me to a table farther away from the tent's entrance.

"Please…I don't want to ruin this day."

"Nothing could, Luisa. I married the love of my life, and you were my maid of honor." She squeezed my fingers. "If Press knew—"

I shook my head. "Please don't," I whispered as Ridge joined us, carrying three glasses of champagne.

"Ladies," he said, handing each of us a glass.

"I probably shouldn't," I said, biting my lip.

"Give it a try," Ridge suggested, winking.

I lifted it and took a sip. Instead of wine, it was sparkling cider.

"I figured it would slow us down so we could enjoy tomorrow as much as today," he added.

I finished what was in my glass. "Wise man."

"I also figured it was better than spitting." Both my sister and I laughed at his reference to the way wine-makers kept from getting drunk on the job when they tasted from barrel after barrel to check on whether the wine was ready to be bottled.

Ridge stood, leaned over, and kissed Seraphina's cheek. "Be right back."

I looked over to where Press, Beau, Zin, and Brix waited just outside the tent. Before Ridge got to them, Tryst did.

I closed my eyes, continued regulating my breathing, and said a prayer that whatever they were discussing had nothing to do with me.

11

Press

"According to Ares, the intelligence comes from a credible source," my brother said when Ridge and Tryst joined us and we'd walked far enough away from the tent so as not to be overheard.

"What exactly did he say?" Ridge asked.

"First of all, I'm sorry to involve you, especially on your wedding day," Beau said to him. "But Ares believes there's enough of a threat that we need to act."

"Got it. Now, tell me what he said."

"Apparently, Luisa's abduction wasn't random. She was requested specifically. The price offered for her was originally one hundred thousand dollars."

"And now?" asked Tryst.

"It's been upped to a quarter of a million."

"What about Varilla?" Ridge asked. "Has he been questioned about this yet?"

"He confirmed what Ares heard. However, he says he was never informed of the buyer's identity."

After being apprehended, shortly after Luisa disappeared, Manual Varilla—the man responsible for her kidnapping—had turned state's evidence. Given all we'd learned from him thus far, I believed if he knew who the buyer was, he would tell us.

"Tryst, how secure is the ranch?" I asked.

"Under normal circumstances..."

"With the wedding, it would be impossible to ensure it's airtight," Ridge finished Tryst's sentence.

"I'm sorry," Tryst said.

I put my hand on his shoulder. "There's nothing for you to apologize for. No one expected a threat of any kind, let alone at this level."

Ridge lowered his head and shook it. "I hate to say this, but we need to get her out of here."

"I'm sorry," Beau said, repeating Tryst's words.

"I'll make the arrangements." While no one said it, even if anyone else had offered to relocate Luisa, I would've suggested she'd feel more comfortable with me, even over my brother. Her interest in him was romantic in nature. No one doubted she felt safest with me.

"You were planning to go to Napa," Beau reminded me.

"You're welcome to go in my place," I snapped.

My brother's wasn't the only raised brow, but I didn't owe him or anyone else an explanation for my surliness. That Luisa remained in danger was certainly cause enough.

"The main residence will be the most secure for the time being," Tryst offered. "I'll make arrangements to have her things brought from the *casita*."

"Press, I'd like to tell Seraphina and her sister together," said Ridge.

"I wish there were another way," I responded, hating to disrupt the wedding celebration but knowing we had to.

"Luisa's safety is all that matters. If anything were to happen to her, it would destroy my wife."

When he walked away from the group, Zin and I went with him. We were a few yards away from Beau, Brix, and Tryst when Zin put his hand on my shoulder.

"We'll join you in a moment," Zin said to Ridge.

Once there was some distance between him and us, my friend turned to me. "What's going on with you?"

"I would think that would be obvious. I would also think you'd be as troubled as I am, hearing Luisa remains in danger."

"I'm talking about before we received the news, Press, and you know it."

I looked out across the landscape of Tryst's ranch. Every other time I was here, I'd been filled with a sense of peace from the moment I arrived. This visit had been entirely different. "She's in love with Beau."

"Not quite the way I'd describe her feelings for him."

I turned to study him. "What do you mean?"

"It's a crush, at best."

This time, I rolled my eyes. "You haven't spent as much time with the two of them as I have."

Zin shook his head. "He's safe."

"I beg to differ. *I'm* safe."

"You're looking at it wrong."

I felt my shoulders tense. I was not in the mood for a discussion about how the woman I loved was enraptured with my brother instead of me. "We need to get in there."

By the time we reached the tent's entrance, Ridge was leading Seraphina and Luisa in our direction.

"We're needed in the chapel," he said. "All of us."

When she approached me, I tucked Luisa's arm in mine and rested my hand on hers. As I expected, neither she nor her sister asked why we were needed at the place where, a short time ago, a wedding ceremony had taken place.

"What's going on?" Seraphina said to Ridge once we were inside the building.

"We've received some news," he began.

I turned to face Luisa and took both her hands in mine. "We've learned of a potential threat."

Like earlier, her eyes filled with tears.

"As hard as it is to suggest this, we think it would be best if you were to leave Mexico," said Ridge.

"When?" she whispered to me.

"Right away," I responded.

"Right away, meaning today?" Seraphina asked.

"I'm sorry, but yes, today." Ridge embraced his wife.

I refocused my gaze on the woman whose hands I still held. When she nodded and took a step closer, I gathered her in my arms like Ridge had with Seraphina. "I'm sorry," I whispered.

After several seconds, Luisa pulled away, approached her sister, and the two women hugged. When they let go, Luisa faced me. I held my hand out, and she took it.

"Tell me what I need to do, Press."

"You and I will join Tryst at the main residence. There, I'll make the necessary arrangements."

"For me to leave?"

"My intention is to accompany you."

"Thank you," she said just above a whisper.

"Do you want Mom to go with you?" Seraphina asked. Luisa looked at me.

"It's up to you," I said.

She shook her head. "I don't want her to have to leave the wedding celebration."

"I can always arrange for her to join us later," I offered.

"I should pack."

"Tryst made arrangements for your belongings to be taken to the main residence," said Zin.

My eyes met his. My anxiety level was already skyrocketing. I wanted to whisk Luisa directly to the plane my brother and I owned jointly. It was sitting on Tryst's private runway since we'd used it to transport many of the wedding guests here from the Central Coast of California. However, it was rated for two pilots, not one, which meant my brother would have to fly with me.

"I'll copilot," Zin offered as though he'd read my mind.

"Would you like Beau to travel with us?" I asked Luisa.

"Is it necessary? I mean, I'd hate for him to have to leave the wedding too. I'm sorry anyone has to because of me."

"To answer your question, it won't be necessary for Beau to go with us if Zin does."

"Then, no."

I had to admit her response stunned me. While staying at Seahorse, and even when she'd relocated to Butler Ranch, one of the first questions Luisa posed when she and I spoke was always about Beau. Where he was, when he might arrive, what he was up to, whether "his friend" was still in town. More often than not, I answered honestly, saying I had no idea. My brother came and went as he pleased, usually without a care as to how it might affect other people.

"How soon will you leave?" Seraphina asked.

Rather than respond, I waited to allow Luisa to answer. Instead of doing so, she turned to me.

"Given the number of additional people on the ranch today to assist with the wedding, it is more difficult for us to ensure your safety."

"I understand. I'd like time to change," she said, motioning to her gown.

"Of course."

When the chapel door, which I'd watched Zin lock, opened, the five of us froze.

"Forgive me," said Tryst. "I should've alerted you of my arrival. I have the SUV waiting outside."

Zin stepped closer to me when Luisa and Seraphina embraced once more. "It might be a good idea to have someone accompany us, given both you and I will be in the cockpit," he whispered.

He was right. The flight time would be at least three hours. While I had no doubt she'd manage, I hated the idea of leaving Luisa alone in the main cabin for that length of time.

Tryst motioned us to the back of the chapel. "There may be someone available to accompany you."

"Who?" I asked.

"Her name is Jaicon Heart—code name Esencia. Merrigan Butler from K19 Security Solutions brought her in to assist with the reunification of the other trafficking victims and their families. She is a former MI6 agent."

"Is she in the area?"

He nodded. "She is, and she has a CMEL rating."

The acronym Tryst referred to stood for a pilot's Commercial Multi-Engine License, which meant Ms. Heart could also fly the plane if necessary.

I would make the offer for Zin to remain in Mexico; however, that wouldn't solve our dilemma of having someone in the cabin with Luisa.

"If she is available and willing, the support would be appreciated. Shall I follow up with Merrigan directly?"

"It's already been taken care of."

"Many thanks," I said, shaking Tryst's hand. I glanced over my shoulder and saw Luisa approaching.

"I'm ready to leave whenever you are."

Ridge and Seraphina walked up behind her. I embraced them both without reiterating the apologies already spoken. Like me, I was certain they were thankful we hadn't received the news about the danger Luisa was in prior to the ceremony.

When we stepped outside, a woman who didn't appear much older than Luisa, was waiting. Tryst introduced her as Jaicon.

"Hello, Luisa," she said, stepping forward to shake her hand. The warm way she greeted her endeared the woman to me immediately. Zin nudged me from behind and motioned in Tryst's direction.

"What do you make of that?" he whispered.

"Not sure," I responded, also whispering. The look on Tryst's face was a mix of pride and admiration, but there appeared to be something more. I was ashamed to admit the disparity in their ages left me questioning whether it was attraction.

Once we were at the main house, Luisa, Zin, and I changed out of our wedding attire, then I worked on filing our flight plan. While it wasn't completely necessary, in order to fly above ten thousand feet using instrument flight rules rather than visual flight rules, filing was required. Prior to finalizing it, though, I needed to speak with Luisa.

"A moment?" I said when she came out of the bedroom where she'd changed.

She approached, and I led her out to the solarium, where we might have a bit of privacy.

"First, you haven't asked the specifics of the threat," I said once we'd both taken a seat on the sofa.

"I'm not sure I want to know yet."

I nodded. "You needn't, then. I assure you, you will be kept safe."

Luisa moved closer to me and rested her head on my shoulder. "I know that, Press."

Her confidence in me was humbling, and I would never take it lightly. "I have a proposal for you."

She raised her head. "What?"

"Rather than immediately return to Seahorse, I was wondering if you'd like to pay a visit to my parents' estate in Napa. The security there is equal to mine." Something else occurred to me. "Unless, of course, you'd prefer to return to Butler Ranch." I assumed that would be okay with Laird and Sorcha Butler, but I would confirm it with them if that was her choice.

"I've never been to Napa."

I leaned over and kissed her temple, something I did out of habit. "If you're interested, I'm sure my parents will adore you…err…our visit." I held my breath, waiting for her to ask about Beau.

"If you're sure I wouldn't be imposing."

"Not at all. I should finalize our flight plan," I said after a long enough time had passed without her asking the question I dreaded.

"Jaicon said she'd be traveling with us."

"Are you comfortable with her doing so?"

Her eyes bored into mine. "I am as long as you…"

I sat back down beside her. "As long as I what?"

She shook her head, and her eyes filled with tears.

"Tell me, pet." I closed my own eyes, reprimanding myself for using an expression she didn't like. "Sorry," I muttered.

"Earlier, you seemed…distant."

I wrapped my arm around her shoulders. "There are times I feel as though I'm smothering you with my overprotective nature. I thought to give you space, not make you feel abandoned."

"If I want space, I'll let you know."

"Noted," I said, standing for the second time. I couldn't help but make the supposition that as soon as my brother showed his face, either in Napa or once we returned to Seahorse, my close presence would no longer be required.

We were in the air a little more than an hour when Jaicon entered the cockpit.

"Everything all right?" I asked.

"I thought perhaps you'd like to take a break. More for Luisa's sake than your own."

My eyes opened wide, and I looked over at Zin, who nodded. I hurried around her, confused when I saw Luisa sitting comfortably, thumbing through a magazine.

"Hi," she said, looking up when I took a seat across from her.

"Hi."

"Um, do you have to get back?" she motioned to the cockpit.

"Not right away if you need something. Jaicon is also a pilot."

"She is?"

"Yes."

"Does that mean you can stay out here with me, at least for a little while?"

"As long as you'd like, actually."

She leaned forward. "Tell me about your parents."

"*My parents.* Well, my mum will be thrilled I'm coming for a visit, particularly since I'm bringing guests. They'll be equally excited to finally meet you."

"Oh. Um, what do they know? I mean, have you spoken to them about…you know?"

"If you mean about your ordeal, I have not. However, they are aware of Ridge and Seraphina's wedding and that the bride has a delightful sister who I, um, and Beau, consider a friend."

Luisa's eyes scrunched. Had she also winced? God, I hated how often I felt I had to measure my words when I spoke with her. Did saying Beau regarded her as a friend offend her? Disappoint her?

Based on her expression, something was clearly amiss. I was about to ask what when she got up and sat in the seat beside me.

12

Luisa

"You're probably wondering why I'm not asking about the threat against me," I said, feeling as though I needed to be close to Press in order to discuss it at all.

"I'm not," he responded.

I studied him. "Why aren't you?"

Like he often did, Press took my hand in the same way I imagined my father would if he were still alive. Actually, maybe not *my* father, but one who was close to his children.

"We don't have to talk about it until you're ready."

I rested my head on his shoulder like I had in the sunroom in Tryst's house. "You're always so patient with me."

"I cannot imagine a reason I wouldn't be."

I raised my head. "You weren't earlier."

He sighed and closed his eyes. "My apologies," he said when he reopened them.

"I'll accept them if you tell me why you were acting the way you were."

Press gave me a sidelong glance. "I believe I already have done."

"Look me in the eye and tell me the *excuse* you gave me was the real reason behind your behavior."

"Have you and Seraphina always gotten along?"

I laughed. "I'm not sure what that has to do with it, but definitely not."

"My irritation was far more with my brother than you. Again, I apologize for making you think otherwise."

"What was he doing to irritate you?"

"Breathing," he muttered.

I laughed a second time. "I'm familiar with the feeling."

He raised a brow.

"I mean with Seraphina. I think she felt that way with me more than I did with her."

"Luisa…"

"The threat." I hadn't allowed my mind to wander with what it might be, and as much as I'd rather not know, I had to.

Press nodded. "As I said, we don't have to discuss it now. Eventually, though, you should be aware."

I took a deep breath. "Tell me."

He studied me, perhaps for any sign of hesitation. "You're certain?"

I hoped my voice didn't waver, revealing my trepidation. "Yes."

Press took both my hands in his. "There is reason to believe your abduction wasn't random. Meaning, you were targeted specifically."

"By Jorge, err, Manual Varilla?"

"No." He hesitated and gripped my hands tighter. "By someone who offered a great deal of money to make it happen."

I felt my stomach lurch. "Who?"

"We don't know, which is why the threat remains."

"Someone wanted to…" I couldn't say the words out loud. *Buy me?* "Me specifically?" Who would do something like that? Who even knew me? I was nobody. "I don't understand."

"Given the amount"—he cleared his throat—"*offered* increased significantly, it appears the individual has not given up."

"Oh my God." I rested my head against the seat. "This really happens?"

"Admittedly, I know very little about human trafficking, but it does. On what level? Again, I'm not certain."

I wished I could rewind the clock and be in the chapel on Tryst's ranch, watching my sister marry Ridge, while the most important thing I had to worry about was that Seraphina had the happiest day of her life. Instead, I was on a plane. I didn't even get to watch her first dance with my brother-in-law or them cut the cake or just marvel that they'd found each other.

Press caressed the back of my hand with his thumb. "I wish I could make all this go away."

I plastered on the same fake smile I had earlier with my sister. "I'm just feeling sorry for myself."

"Luisa—"

"Thanks to you and everyone else who showed up at the port outside London, I'm alive, and so are many others." I ran my hand over the supple leather of the plane's seat. "I'm in a private jet on my way to an estate in Napa Valley, where I'll spend the rest of Christmas with someone who has become one of my dearest friends."

"You amaze me, darling Luisa—your bravery, your tenacity. I admire you so."

I must've fallen asleep resting my head on Press' shoulder, but woke when he tried to ease away from me.

"My apologies. I should return to the cockpit. We'll be landing soon."

"Of course," I said, sitting up and stretching. "I'm sorry I fell asleep."

"We'll be on the ground soon. Once we've landed, it will take us approximately one hour to get to my parents' place."

"Okay," I said, scooting over to look out the window.

"How are you holding up?" Jaicon asked, joining me in the main cabin a couple of minutes later.

"Okay. Thanks."

"Press mentioned he informed you of the reason we left Mexico. If you have any questions or concerns, I'm available at any time."

"Thanks, Jaicon."

"And please, call me Jacy."

"Again, thank you, Jacy. So, um, Press said you used to work for MI6."

"I did."

"Do you miss it?"

"What I do now isn't terribly different. I'd once hoped to work with Fatale. You probably know her as Merrigan. Anyway, I expected she'd take over as chief. When she passed on the job, I was quite disappointed, to be honest. Working with her now makes up for it."

"Wait, I remember Merrigan saying she left MI6 a few years ago."

Jacy cocked her head. "Yes."

"A *few* years ago, I was still in high school. You don't appear to be much older than me."

"Thank you, but if that's the case, I'm considerably older than you are." She smiled. "I do hear that quite often. I've my mother to thank for my youthful appearance. The downside when I go out in the States is I've been accused of having a forged identification card."

I chuckled and stared out the window. "Looks like we'll be landing soon."

"In advance of that, I'd like to brief you on what to expect."

I turned my head toward her.

"A team will be joining us when we land at the Napa airfield. They will remain on your detail as long as necessary. It is unlikely you will be aware of their presence. However, you'll be meeting them upon our arrival." Jacy handed me a cell phone. "I've programmed the necessary numbers into your new phone, including your sister's and mother's."

"What about Jada? She's my best friend."

"Ah, Yáñez, correct?"

"Yes."

"Sorry. I forgot she was cleared." Jacy swiped the screen and appeared to be entering contact information.

"You know her number?"

She nodded. "I'm afraid I've a photographic memory."

"That would've been useful when I was getting my MBA."

She smiled. "There are times it's a curse as much as a blessing."

"Prepare for landing," Zin said from the cockpit. "We'll be on the ground in under ten minutes."

While I'd traveled via private plane a few times in the last few weeks, I doubted I'd ever get used to looking out the window to see vehicles parked and waiting for our arrival.

When Jacy stood, I did too and followed her toward the front of the plane, where Zin was lowering the stairs we'd use to deboard.

"I'd like to wait for Press," I said when he motioned for me to follow Jacy.

"I'm here," he said, stepping up behind me. "Did Jacy brief you on the team meeting us?" he asked.

"She did."

"I've not met any of them either, but if they're part of the K19 crew, I'm sure they're very good at what they do."

With wide eyes, I watched five men pile out of the two SUVs parked within several yards of us. One of them, who appeared older than the others, stepped forward first.

"Luisa, I'd like to introduce Patton Abrams," said Jacy.

He shook my hand. "Most people call me Tank, ma'am." There was no question as to why they did. The man was built like an armored vehicle.

"And this is Lavery Barrett, aka Press, and Vaile Oliver, who most call Zin," Jacy continued, motioning Tank over to them.

Another man approached. "I'm Henry Bonham, code name Zeppelin, and this here is Magnet, uh, Justin…"

"Magnussen. I'm your best friend, and you don't know my bloody last name?" He slugged Zeppelin's arm. "Nice to meet you, miss."

While Tank sounded American, the other two were definitely European.

Magnet pointed to the men who appeared to be surveilling our surroundings. "That's Atticus and Blackjack. You'll meet them later."

"Where are they from?" I asked.

"Both from the Bay area," said Tank. "Like me."

"We're the only imports besides Jaicon," added Zeppelin.

"Where do you want me?" Zin asked.

"You can ride with us in the second vehicle," Magnet told him.

"I'll grab the bags," Press offered.

"If you'll take Miss Reeve to the first SUV, we'll handle getting your gear," said Tank.

"This is intense," I whispered once we'd gotten into the backseat.

"Precious cargo," said Press, resting his hand on mine.

"I don't think I'm worth all this." I motioned with my hand toward the plane.

"There are a few of us who obviously disagree," he said, squeezing my fingers and winking.

"How far is it to your parents' house?" I remembered him telling me, but I couldn't recall what he'd said.

"Approximately an hour. It depends on how quickly we can get through the valley. Most of the wineries are open for tasting, so there may be traffic. However, the majority will be going in the opposite direction."

"On Christmas?"

"Like for theme parks, this is one of their busier days."

"This is odd."

I woke with a start and looked around. "What?" I asked Press.

His forehead scrunched. "The gate is open."

"Get a vector," I heard Zeppelin, who was seated in the front passenger seat, say. A few moments later, the second SUV drove around us and through the gate.

The sun had set, but there were no lights, so I couldn't see anything beyond several trees that lined the driveway.

"Roger that," Zeppelin said several minutes later. Magnet, who was behind the wheel, went in the direction the first vehicle had.

"What's happening?" Press asked.

"We'll know more in a minute, but Tank gave us the all clear."

We slowly made our way down the long driveway until we reached the house. Magnet pulled up under the portico, where the other vehicle's passengers were standing near the front door, talking with an older-looking woman.

"Go ahead," I said to Press when he turned to me.

He got out and rushed over. At the same time, Zeppelin opened my door.

"Oh, Mr. Lavery," I heard the woman say. "They took your mother by helicopter. Your father went with her."

Press held his phone to his ear. "He's not answering. Which hospital?" he asked the woman.

"St. Helena."

"How long ago did they leave?"

"Fifteen minutes ago," she responded, checking her watch.

Press turned to me. "I'm sorry. I have to join my parents at the hospital."

"Don't apologize. Just go."

"I'll drive," said Magnet as the two men raced back to the SUV.

"Let's go inside," said Jacy, leading me into the house.

13

Press

I checked for missed calls, then rang my brother.

"Press?" he answered. "Are you home?"

"Something's happened to Mum—"

"Wait. I can't hear you over the music. Let me get outside. Okay. Go ahead."

"I just arrived at the house. Mrs. Gonzales said our mother was taken to the hospital via helicopter. Father went with her. I'm on my way now."

"Oh, God. I knew I should've come with you. I'll make arrangements to leave now."

Knowing I'd have news long before he could arrange for a flight, I didn't bother telling him to hold off. "I'll ring back as soon as I know something."

"Thanks, Press, and I'm so sorry."

I ended the call and tried my father a second time, to no avail.

Magnet pulled up to the emergency room entrance. "Thanks," I said, jumping out and racing inside.

"Can I help you?" a woman sitting behind a counter just inside the doors asked.

"My mother was brought here via helicopter."

"Name?"

"Susannah Barrett. My father, Martin Barrett, is with her."

"Take a seat and I'll check."

"Take a seat?"

She picked up a phone but didn't place a call. "Yes, sir. Please."

I walked several feet away but had no intention of sitting down.

"Sir?" I heard her say a few seconds later. I approached. "Someone will be out to speak with you in a few minutes."

"I'm her son. Why am I not permitted to join my father?"

"Only one visitor per patient, sir."

"I'm hardly a *visitor*. As I said, I'm her son."

"Hospital policy, sir."

When she lowered her gaze as if to dismiss me, I walked over to the windows lining the waiting area. I was about to ring Beau to tell him I still didn't know anything when I heard my name called.

"I'm Lavery Barrett," I said, approaching a man dressed in scrubs who stood directly outside a set of double doors.

"Come with me, sir."

I followed him past several bays and around a corner. He opened a door. Inside, I saw my father sitting with his head in his hands. The man shut the door behind me, leaving us alone.

"Dad?"

When he looked up, I saw he was crying.

"Lavery? How…"

"I came home early. I wanted to surprise you and Mum. How is she? What's happened?"

He leaned forward, covered his face again, and sobbed.

I knelt in front of him and put my hand on his shoulder. "Dad? Please…"

"She's…"—his voice broke—"gone."

Gone? It couldn't possibly be…No, I refused to even consider it. "What do you mean?"

"I'm sorry," he cried. "I just…"

I put my arms around my dad and held him as he cried, tears running down my own cheeks.

We remained that way for several minutes. Finally, my father pulled away and sat upright. "They're not sure what happened," he said, wiping his face with a handkerchief. "There was nothing they could do."

"Can you explain what took place at the house?"

"She and I were in the kitchen. Your mother opened the refrigerator door and just collapsed. I tried…" My father's voice broke again.

"It's okay, Dad. Take your time."

"I couldn't find a pulse," he said after taking several deep breaths. "I tried CPR. Mrs. Gonzales called 911."

There was a knock at the door. When I stood and opened it, a man who introduced himself as Dr. Shammas joined us. "I'm very sorry for your loss, Mr. Barrett," he said, placing his hand on my father's shoulder like I had.

"I'm Lavery Barrett. Their son," I said.

"I'm sorry, Lavery," the doctor said to me.

"What happened?"

"We're not entirely certain, but we suspect your mother may have had a pulmonary embolism that traveled to her heart. While mortality rates are low, approximately ten percent of people who suffer from this occurrence do not survive." He turned to my father. "Had your wife complained of shortness of breath? Pain?"

My dad shook his head.

"Given we're uncertain of the cause of death, we'd like to perform an autopsy. It is your decision whether we do so or not. You do not need to make the determination right away. However, the results will be more conclusive if it's done within the first twenty-four hours."

"Was Mum an organ donor?" I asked my father.

"She was."

"I'm afraid it's too late for her organs to be viable." The doctor put his hand on the doorknob. "I'll give you some time to talk it over," he said before leaving the room.

"It won't bring her back," my dad said, looking up at me.

"It will not."

His eyes bored into mine. "I don't know what to do."

"We need to let Beau know what's happened."

"Yes." When my father put his head in his hands for the third time, I stepped out of the room.

"Is there a place I can make a call? I need to alert my brother," I approached a desk and asked.

"Of course. Come with me." A woman, also dressed in scrubs, stood and led me to a room that looked similar to the one my father was in. I took several deep breaths after she shut the door behind me, trying to muster the courage to call Beau, knowing there would be no easy way to tell him our beloved mum was gone.

After speaking with my brother, my father and I decided against an autopsy. As Dad had said, knowing her cause of death would not bring her back.

Tryst was able to make arrangements for Beau to get a flight with someone he knew who also owned a private jet and lived nearby. "You stay with Dad. I'll get a car service," he said when I offered to meet him at the airfield.

The next call I placed was to Zin.

"Jesus, Press. I'm so sorry. I don't know what to say. What can I do?" he asked after I told him the news.

"My father and I will be leaving the hospital. Do you know if Magnet returned to the house?"

"Negative. He's still there, waiting."

"If someone could make contact and let him know we're ready to go, I'd appreciate it."

"Roger that. What about Luisa? Do you want me to tell her, or would you rather speak to her yourself?"

I checked the time. It was close to midnight. "Don't wake her."

"She's not asleep, Press. No one is. We've all been waiting to hear from you."

"It's best you inform everyone before my father and I return."

"Will do. What about sleeping arrangements? We're in the main house now, but we can move to one of the guesthouses."

In terms of security, they were all equal to the main residence. "Perhaps that would be best. My father—"

"Say no more. I'll take care of it. Tomorrow, we'll talk about relocating."

Relocating? I supposed it might be necessary, given what the following few days would bring. "Don't make any arrangements to do so until I've seen Luisa."

"Of course not, Press."

We'd been at the house under an hour when my father said the doctor had given him something to take for sleep. After we embraced, he went upstairs to the suite he and my mother had shared.

Even if I had something to take, I wouldn't have done. It didn't matter that Luisa had more than enough security to ensure her safety; that she was in a guesthouse rather than here with me left me feeling unsettled.

I poured a glass of brandy from the bottle my father kept in his study and walked over to the window. From there, I could see lights on in the house where Luisa slept. I was about to turn away when I saw her figure appear in the window. She raised her hand, and I did the same. Seconds later, my mobile rang.

"You should be asleep," I said.

"Press, I'm so sorry."

"Thank you, Luisa." I'd wept briefly after speaking with my brother, but now, I felt on the brink of doing so again.

"I wish there was something I could do."

I tried to respond, to thank and assure her I'd be fine, but my voice broke.

"Press—"

I hung my head, knowing there'd be no way for me to stop the tears that had begun to flow. When I raised my eyes seconds later, Luisa was walking across the lawn—accompanied by Jacy and Zin—headed toward the main house. I met her at the front door.

"Press," she repeated, rushing over to embrace me. "I'll only leave if you tell me to," she whispered, tightening her arms around me.

I shook my head. Right or wrong, I needed her comfort. "It's okay," I said, my eyes meeting Zin's.

"The house is secure," Jaicon said before Zin escorted her outside and closed the door behind them.

I led Luisa to the room that had always been my mother's favorite. It had once been a southern-facing veranda, but my father had arranged for it to be enclosed and for a fireplace to be added so she was comfortable in it regardless of the weather. During the day, there was a sweeping view of the vineyards from this room.

Once there, Luisa took my hand and led me over to the daybed where my mum had often napped.

She lay on it and held her hand out to me. When I stretched out beside her, Luisa put her head on my chest and her arm around my waist.

I woke in the same position several hours later, based on how high the sun was in the sky.

"Press?" I heard my brother whisper.

I raised my head, eased Luisa onto the pillow, and got up, following my brother far enough into another part of the house that we wouldn't wake her. Then we embraced.

"How's Dad?" he asked.

"Still resting, I hope." I studied him. His eyes were as bloodshot as I expected mine were. "When did you arrive?"

"About fifteen minutes ago. Zin picked me up at the airfield at nine."

I followed my brother into the kitchen and motioned for him to be seated at the table while I made us both an espresso. "I figured we could both use something stronger than tea this morning," I said, setting the cup in front of him. I also knew it was Beau's preference.

"Soon, we'll need something heartier than this," he said, bringing the cup to his lips and softly blowing on the steaming liquid. "Tell me again what the doctors said."

"That it was likely a pulmonary embolism that traveled from her lungs to her heart. I'm not certain what led them to believe so."

"How's Luisa?"

"Likely far more concerned about us than herself."

Beau nodded. "Do you think it's a good idea for her to stay here?"

I shrugged. "Zin said something similar last night. Probably not." I hated the idea of not being with her, but my father needed me more than she did. There were decisions to be made regarding a memorial service, and given my parents were deeply entrenched in the community—particularly with other vineyard owners—there would likely be people coming and going over the course of the next several days.

"Everyone is trying to get here later today."

"Who do you mean by everyone?"

"Los Caballeros."

"It isn't necessary for Ridge to come—"

Beau shook his head. "Are you telling me that if Ridge lost one of his parents, you wouldn't drop everything to be there for him?"

His question was rhetorical. And he was right. Nothing would keep me away. While we weren't all brothers by blood, those of us who were part of Los Caballeros considered each other as such.

"Hi," I heard Luisa say as she walked into the kitchen. Both Beau and I stood, and she embraced him like she had me the night before. "I'm so sorry about your mother."

"Thank you," he said, stepping back and motioning for her to take his chair.

"Can I get you a coffee?" I asked.

She put her hand on my arm. "Let me do it," she said, her eyes meeting mine as she leaned closer. "Let me take care of you for a change."

My brother and I retook our seats without argument. I'd woken when Beau whispered my name, feeling as exhausted and overwrought as I had when I lay beside Luisa after returning from the hospital. I had no idea what the day would bring, but I knew it would be draining.

14

Luisa

"I want to talk to Press first," I said to Zin the following day when he told me he'd made arrangements for me to return to Butler Ranch, where my mother and I had been staying prior to Seraphina's wedding.

"He's got his hands full with the memorial service—"

"I want to be here for him and Beau. I want to help them. I'll stay out of the way except for when one of them needs me."

He sighed and looked in the direction of the main house.

Something occurred to me. "Did Press say he wanted me to leave?" I asked.

He shook his head. "No, but I know he's worried about you when he should be focusing his energy on himself and his family."

Zin's words stung, but put that way, I knew he was right.

"Okay. I'll go."

"It's for the best, Luisa. Let him get through this without distractions."

"I said I'll go." I folded my arms and walked away. "I can be ready to leave in ten minutes." I went into the bedroom. Truthfully, I could be ready in less time than that. I hadn't unpacked more than a change of clothes and my toiletries. I tossed everything into my suitcase and was wheeling it into the main room when Press walked in the front door.

"Where are you going?" he asked.

"Butler Ranch," Zin answered before I could.

Press looked from me to him. "Give us a few minutes, please."

"We're scheduled to leave in fifteen," he said, walking out the door Press had come through.

"It's for the best," I said when he walked toward me. "You and Beau need to focus on yourselves and your family without distractions."

He stopped in front of me. "That's Zin talking."

"Yes, but he's right."

"Have either of you considered I'll be more distracted if I can't see for myself that you're safe?"

"There's practically an army making sure I am."

I looked over Press' shoulder and saw Beau headed in our direction. He turned and looked too.

"How is he?" I asked when Press faced me again.

"Same as my father, I suppose. Apart from when we were at the hospital, I haven't seen either of them break down." Press took a step closer. "If you feel at all uncomfortable about leaving, I want you to know you don't have to."

"I know, I just—oh my God—he *punched* him!"

Press spun around in time to see Zin stumbling backwards and Beau shaking his right fist. It appeared he was yelling at him.

"Excuse me," said Press, racing out the door with me right behind him. *"What in the bloody hell?"*

"Do you know he's making her leave? Are you part of this?" Beau shouted at his brother.

I rushed forward and got to him before Press did. "If you're talking about me, no one is making me do anything."

"I don't want you to leave," Beau cried, gathering me in his arms. I could feel the dampness of his tears against my own face. From where we stood, I could see both Press' and Zin's confused expressions.

"Let's go for a walk," I said, taking his hand in mine. "We'll be back in a few minutes." I didn't wonder if it was okay with anyone if we did so. Jacy had reminded me more than once that, regardless of whether I could see them or not, there were six people watching over me. They only took shifts at night, when I was asleep.

The other thing I knew was that, similar to Seahorse, Press' parents' estate was as secure as the White House. Maybe more so. However, like at the wedding, it would be impossible to vet every person who came onto the property to pay their respects to Susannah Barrett and her family.

"Beau?" I said once we were far enough away that Press and Zin couldn't hear us. "What was that about?"

He led me to a bench under a willow tree. We sat in silence for a few minutes before he spoke. "To be honest, I don't know. I just feel as though…"

I put my hand on his and gave him time to gather his thoughts.

"Alone. That's how I feel. Alone. My mum, well, she was…"

When he tried to hide that he was crying, I rubbed his back. "Let it out, Beau. There's no judgment here."

He turned his body, and we embraced.

"I'm sorry," he said a few minutes later, pulling away.

"Please don't be. We all need to allow ourselves to *feel*."

"If you want to leave, I understand."

"It isn't that I want to; it's more that I believe it's the best for all concerned. You and Press must focus on your family, on your father. To mourn the loss of your mother."

"You don't have to leave in order for us to do that."

"I do, Beau. There are people watching us now. They're watching me all the time. If someone who was out to harm me came on the property pretending to be one of your guests, I can't say what that would look like. I'd hate for me to be the cause of such a disruption."

He took a deep breath. "I need you."

I closed my eyes and raised my face to the sun. There'd been a time hearing those words would have meant everything to me. But then, when his girl-friend—or whatever she was to him—had shown up at Seahorse from Australia, he seemed to forget I existed. I wondered if she—Daphne—was on her way here now. Perhaps she'd even arrive sometime today. In which case, like before, Beau would forget I existed. I stopped myself from saying it out of fear the jealousy I felt would be evident.

"We should get back." He stood, held his hand out to me, and pulled me into an embrace. "Thank you."

"Of course."

When we got close enough to see the guesthouse, Press and Zin were seated on the porch. The two SUVs that caravaned from the airport were parked out front.

"Are you leaving now?" Beau asked.

"I am."

He stopped walking, and since he still held my hand in his, I did too. He put his arms around me in what I thought was another embrace, except this time he did something he never had before. Beau kissed me.

I'd lost count of the number of nights I fell to sleep fantasizing about the first time he would. It felt nothing like I thought it would. Maybe it was the timing of it, but it felt wrong. Particularly given our audience.

"Sorry," he said when I pulled away. "I just needed…"

"It's okay."

When I raised my head and looked in the direction of the guesthouse, Zin still sat on the porch but the seat where Press had been was empty.

"Ready?" Zin asked when I approached.

"Where's Press?"

"He was needed at the main house."

"Oh, I, um, wanted to say goodbye."

"It's unnecessary. He knows you're leaving."

"Are you going with me?" I asked him.

"I'm needed here."

I didn't say it, but I was glad. It was evident Zin didn't like me, and the feeling had become mutual.

Jacy was standing near the second SUV, and I walked over to her. "Where do you want me?"

"You and I will ride together," she said, opening the door. I climbed in and saw my purse on the backseat. I had no doubt my bag had also been loaded into the vehicle.

As we drove past the main house, I could see Press standing near one of the windows, looking in our direction. I raised my hand, but he didn't.

It was a five-hour drive from Napa Valley to Paso Robles, where Butler Ranch was located. I slept most of the way. Riding in a car always made me drowsy. My sister was the same way. Thinking of her reminded me I'd only spoken to her once since I left Mexico. Maybe once we arrived at the ranch and I had some privacy, I'd try calling her again. My mom too.

"They're here!" I gasped after we'd driven through the ranch's gates and up to the main house. Seraphina, my mom, and Jada Yáñez were sitting on the front porch, talking with Sorcha Butler. As soon as the SUV stopped, I jumped out, raced over, and hugged each of the four women.

"I'm so happy to see you," I said, brushing away my tears.

"Oh, lass. Don't cry now," said Sorcha, hugging me a second time. She pulled back and looked me up and down. "Haven't they been feedin' you?"

I laughed. "Sorcha, if I left it to you, I'd eat nonstop all day."

"Come inside. We've a late lunch ready." She glanced over her shoulder. "Although, looking at those brutes, I wonder if there'll be enough food."

"There's always more than enough food, no matter how many people show up," I said, putting my arm through hers.

"Not the size of them."

I smiled and looked over at Jada. She and I used to be together all day, every day. Joined at the hip, as they say. In the last couple of years, we'd hardly seen each other at all. I let go of Sorcha's arm and waited for my best friend to catch up with me.

"I'm so happy you're here."

Jada smiled. "No place I'd rather be. How are you holding up?"

I led her over to the sofa, and we sat beside each other. "It's surreal. Ya know?"

"Actually, I don't." She smiled and shrugged. "All my brother said was there was a threat. I guess I'm not ranked high enough for need-to-know."

I leaned closer. "From what I've been told, someone wanted me specifically," I whispered.

Jada's eyes opened wide. "Oh my God," she mouthed. "So that's why they're here?" She pointed to the two men standing near the door, one outside, one in.

"Yep, and there are three more of them, plus Jaicon."

Her cheeks flushed.

"What?" I asked.

"I haven't seen the other three, but those two are *hot*."

I shrugged. "I hadn't really noticed."

"Still got it bad for Beau Barrett?"

Did I? It wasn't as though he'd been around to distract me from how good-looking my team of bodyguards was. Maybe I just hadn't been in the mood to notice. Even now, though, they didn't do it for me. "I guess," I finally said. "It could also be the circumstances."

"Of course. You're right. I'm sorry."

I leaned into her. "Don't be. I really need a sense of normalcy."

"I was so sorry to hear about Mrs. Barrett. She was always so nice whenever I saw her."

"I don't remember ever meeting her." The thought left me feeling bereft.

"I only saw her at the Wicked Winemakers' Ball, when I volunteered to help."

"I forgot you used to do that." Alex Avila-Butler, who ran the fundraiser, was Jada's cousin. Their mothers were twins.

"I was too busy with school this year, but I heard she bid on both her sons in the bachelor auction."

I raised a brow. "She did?"

"That's the saddest part. Alex said she did it because she never got to spend time with them."

I closed my eyes and hung my head. That was partly my fault. At least in the last two months. Seraphina told me Ridge, Press, Beau, and the others had gotten involved to help find me the night of the very auction Jada was talking about. The only reason Press and Beau hadn't seen their parents at Thanksgiving was because their mother and father spent the holiday in London, and by then, we'd returned to the States. While they'd never said so, it wouldn't surprise me to learn the Barrett boys stuck around Paso Robles because of me. Maybe not Beau, but definitely Press.

"I should thank Bradley," I said, looking behind me to see her and Sorcha putting food on the big dining room table. She and her husband, Naughton Butler, had lived in the main house since before their baby was born. Sorcha and her husband, Laird, had insisted they preferred to move into one of the smaller cottages Laird had built on the estate, similar to the one my mom and I stayed in before and would again now. However, whenever there was a gathering of people, it was always here.

"She never seems to mind hosting," said Jada, following my gaze.

"I doubt she'd say if she did." While Sorcha was one of the nicest people I'd ever known, she was definitely formidable. I patted Jada's hand and stood. "Be right back."

Bradley and Sorcha had gone into the kitchen, and I followed. "What can I do to help?" I asked.

"Not a thing," said Sorcha, walking out of the room carrying another platter.

"You're a saint for always doing this," I said to Bradley.

She smiled. "The truth is, I love it. As an only child, I always wished for a big family. And I can't complain; Sorcha and Laird do all the work."

"But your house is always overrun."

She smiled again and handed me a platter. "That's the last of it, and I promise it doesn't bother me at all. Naughton loves it too, and Charlie adores having so many people around, especially his grandparents."

"Where's Ridge?" I asked my sister when she walked over to me after I'd deposited the platter on the table.

"On his way to Napa."

"You didn't go with him?"

She shook her head. "Once he told me you were coming here, I decided not to go."

"I hate being such a pain in the ass."

Seraphina nudged me with her elbow. "If that were the case, I would've gone with him."

"What's the honeymoon plan?" I asked.

"We're holding off for now."

"And that's *not* because of me, right?" I rolled my eyes.

"You would do the same."

We both raised our heads when there was a knock at the door and Tryst came inside. "What's he doing here?" I whispered. "You'd think he'd be on his way to Napa too."

"He is, but I guess he wanted to stop here first."

"Why?" I'd no more than asked when I had my answer. Or it seemed that way. Before greeting anyone else, Tryst approached Jacy, and the two went outside. "Did you see that?" I asked Seraphina, who was busy filling her plate with food.

"See what?"

"Nothing. Never mind." Telling her the way Tryst had rested his hand on Jacy's lower back wouldn't be as interesting as if she'd witnessed it herself.

My sister, my mom, Jada, and I were seated at the table, eating, when Jacy came back in alone and approached us. "Tryst said he's sorry for not being able to spend more time here. He had to hurry to catch a flight to Napa. He asked me to inform you he'll be back later this week."

I wondered where I'd be then. More than likely, still here.

15

"You've been avoiding me since Luisa left," said Beau, cornering me in my father's study, where I'd gone to pour myself a brandy.

While we both knew it was a lie, I still denied it. "I've more important matters to attend to."

"I'm her son too."

I stared down my brother. "What's this about? Do you feel as though decisions have been made without your input? There weren't any I'm aware of." I skirted around him, stalked out of the room, and ran straight into Zin. Thankfully, none of the brandy spilled. I brought the glass to my lips and took a drink.

"I'd ask if you were okay, but I know better."

"Leave it alone, mate."

"Now is not the time for the two of you to get into it over Luisa."

My eyes bored into his in the same way they had with my brother. "Watch it, Zin, or you'll find yourself on the receiving end of *my* fist."

"She isn't your responsibility. There's a team of people ensuring her safety. In fact, it might be better if Los Caballeros let K19 take it from here."

"What are you on about?"

"You've spent the last two months following Luisa Reeve around like a puppy dog."

"Sod off, Zin," I spat. I stalked away, but spun around when I felt him on my heels. "I mean it. Get the fuck away from me." I pointed to the door. "You know your way out."

"Press, I'm your best friend. I'm looking out for you. That's it."

"I don't need you or anyone else *looking out* for me. *Leave me alone!*" I hurled my empty glass at the wall, and it shattered. I took the stairs two at a time and was almost to my bedroom door when my father came out of his. I took several deep breaths to calm myself.

"What is going on, Lavery?"

"Sorry, Dad."

He walked over to me and put his hand on my shoulder. "Don't apologize. Tell me what's going on."

"I find myself with a rather short fuse in the face of losing Mum. My apologies. It won't happen again."

My father studied me. "Did you hear what I said?"

"Yes, sir."

"I think not. Come, let's get a drink."

He led me to the suite he and my mother had shared. The door opened to a sitting area. Beyond that was what had been their bedroom, en suite bath, and two walk-in closets, one for each of them. There was a fire burning in the fireplace, and I saw a half-full glass of dark liquid on the table near the chair where he usually sat. He raised it, downed the contents, then walked to a cart near the window that held several bottles of booze, an ice bucket, and three empty glasses. He poured another for himself and one for me, then we both took a seat.

"You and your brother are at odds."

"That wasn't Beau I was arguing with. It was Zin."

"Regardless. You've kept your distance."

I took a sip and studied the flames of the fire.

"Your mother was always able to get through to the two of you. I find myself unable to fill her shoes."

"Perhaps when we were children. We're adults now and able to settle our own differences."

"This is about Luisa Reeve, isn't it?"

I closed my eyes and rested against the chair. "Forgive me. I mean no disrespect, but that is not a conversation I'm willing to have with you or anyone else. Particularly today."

"You care a great deal for her."

"Dad, please."

"If your mother were here, she'd tell you not to do what you've always done."

I opened my eyes and looked at him. "And what is that?"

"Step aside whenever you and your brother desired the same thing. The Jag is a perfect example, as is Sheriff."

"Again, forgive me, Father, but you're speaking of an automobile and a horse. Luisa is—"

"The woman you're in love with."

I finished what was in my glass. "As I said, this is not a conversation I'm willing to participate in."

"I'm going to give you the same advice your mother would if she were with us today. She'd tell you that, this time, you need to step in front of your brother, not to the side."

I stood and walked over to the window. Rather than pour myself another glass, I set it on the table. "There are circumstances that make things difficult."

"I'm aware."

I looked over my shoulder at him.

"Tryst called shortly after you left Mexico, son."

"You knew I was on my way."

My father nodded. "As did your mother."

"I should have called. I'd meant to surprise you. I don't know what I was thinking. It wasn't as though it was a simple visit. My God, I brought a security team with me—" I meant to apologize, but my voice was clogged with emotion. "I've made so many mistakes, Dad. The first was not spending time with her. God, she bid on me at the bachelor auction just so she could have dinner with me."

"That wasn't why she did it."

"That's what she told Alex."

"Yes, but I was there that night."

"Why did she, Dad?"

"She wanted your bids to be the highest. Little did we know Brix had rigged his own to be, or that Ridge's would go as high as it had." My father smiled. "Your mother was ready to throttle him."

"He was a man in love."

"Then Ridge was, and now it's you."

I shook my head. "She's in love with Beau."

"Nonsense." My father stood, set his glass on the cart, like I had, and looked out the window. "Guests will be arriving soon. We should make our way downstairs."

"Of course. Before we do, I want to apologize again and also let you know whatever you need, I'm here for you, Dad."

He put his hand on my shoulder. "That conversation you didn't want to have? That's the kind of thing I need, Lavery. You're my son, and I love you more than anything else in the world. Your mother felt the same way about you and your brother. She'd want me to focus on the two of you, making sure you're okay. Not the other way around."

"I should change," I said, motioning to the door.

My father nodded, and I left the room.

Not knowing when I might have the chance again and wanting to clear the air, I rang Luisa.

"Hi," she answered before I even heard the call connect.

"I trust you made it safely to Butler Ranch."

"Hang on. Let me go outside so I can hear you." I heard a door opening and closing. "Okay, that's better. Yes, I made it safely."

"Let me guess. Sorcha is feeding the masses?"

Luisa chuckled. "You're right. She actually expressed concern there wouldn't be enough food once she saw my *entourage*."

"Tank alone could probably polish off enough for several guests."

"How are you, Press?"

"As well as can be expected. I, um, called to apologize for not being there to send you off."

"Why weren't you?"

"Must I admit to it?" I muttered under my breath, not that it kept her from hearing me.

"I'm sorry. I had no idea he planned—"

"There is no need for you to apologize."

She didn't speak, but I could hear her breathing.

"I've just left a conversation with my father," I said.

"How's he doing?"

"Taking on the role of my mother along with his."

"He's worried about you and Beau. Any parent would be, with the loss of the other."

I cleared my throat when I felt emotion welling up. *I miss you,* I longed to say but couldn't bring myself to do so. "I should, um, go. Guests will be arriving soon."

"Of course. Thank you for calling, Press."

"We'll talk again soon."

"I hope so."

The first person I saw when I came downstairs was Zin. I held out my hand, and he shook it.

"I was out of line," he said.

"You were. Now, let's drop it."

He nodded, and the two of us went into the main room, where my father and brother were seated.

The three of us collectively decided not to have a traditional visitation or a funeral service. Instead, those who wished to pay their respects were invited to the house this afternoon and evening.

Two days from now, we'd have a private service at the graveside here, on the property, where my mother would be buried. Eventually, my father would be too, in the same way his parents, grandparents, and great-grandparents had been. When the time came, I expected my brother and I would be as well.

Shortly before I'd purchased the oceanfront estate in Cambria, Beau and I sat down with our mother and father and told them we'd come to an agreement regarding the Napa Valley property. Eventually, it would be passed down to Beau. He would be responsible for the vineyard and winery production, and the property would become his.

That I'd relinquished my rights was concerning to our parents. I couldn't recall many instances when my mother was as angry with me as she was that day.

"You must stand up for yourself, Lavery. You've been this way since Beau was old enough to demand you give him something that was rightfully yours," she'd said.

I'd argued that I never had the same level of interest in wine-making Beau had, but she didn't buy it.

Still, my mind was made up, and as far as I was concerned, I wouldn't change it. I'd requested my parents change their wills in order to reflect what my brother and I had agreed upon, and to the best of my knowledge, they'd honored it.

Even now, as I surveyed the house where I'd spent some of my childhood, although not its majority, I felt no regret over essentially handing my half of our inheritance over to my brother.

Actually, saying I'd given him my half wasn't remotely accurate. I still managed the business side of our family's holdings, which were vast and required near full-time attention from a staff who reported to me. I also held a trust passed down from my grandparents that ensured I'd never want for money. As did Beau.

Tonight, it hit me more than at any other time in my life. *Money did not buy happiness.* It had not stopped my mother's sudden death. Apart from making sure Luisa was protected by a team of bodyguards, my money could not guarantee she'd never face pain or fear again—the very thing I wished it could ensure.

Hours later, after a parade of people had moved through the house, offering their condolences, telling stories about my mother, eating the food the caterers had prepared, and drinking the wine Beau and my father had made, I sat in a room with my very closest friends in the world.

My father and Tryst were reminiscing about their days with Los Caballeros, while Cru, Cris, Trev, Snapper, and Kick—Brix's brothers—sat talking with Dalton, Ridge's only sibling, and Beau.

Brix and Ridge, both away from their wives far too soon after their weddings, sat and told stories with Zin and me. I wondered if, in the back of their minds, they were thinking as much about Addy and Seraphina as I was about Luisa.

While I accepted it was safer for her to be at Butler Ranch rather than here, I missed her—and my mother—so much it hurt to breathe.

16

Luisa

"I miss you," I'd whispered, staring too long at the phone after our call ended and wishing I'd been brave enough to speak those words when Press could've heard me.

No doubt he would've thought it was silly since it hadn't been an entire day since we last saw each other.

I thought, too, about Beau's kiss earlier. For so long, I'd yearned for it, and when it happened, I felt nothing.

"What are you thinking about?" asked Jada, who'd offered to spend the night rather than drive the two miles down the road to her own house. Now, she was stretched out on the other twin bed in the room she and I had volunteered to share.

"Beau Barrett."

She turned on her side and propped her head on her hand. "He's a player, Luisa. Don't say I didn't warn you."

I sighed. "He kissed me earlier today."

Her eyes opened wide. "I'm sorry to be mean, but didn't his mother just die?"

"Yeah, I mean, he and I had been talking about her. I guess you could say I was comforting him. Then I had to leave. I think he just got caught up in the moment. Ya know?"

"Then what happened?"

"Nothing. I left."

"And now you wish you could talk to him?"

I turned to my side and faced her. "No. It's Press I want to talk to."

"Press? Why?" She shuddered.

I rolled to my back and stared up at the ceiling. "He's not that bad. I mean, he's not bad at all. He's been so kind to me."

"Are we talking about the same person? Lavery Barrett?"

I smiled. "He isn't anything like I thought he was."

"Brix is my cousin, and I love him, but he, Ridge, and Press have always been…"

"A lot older than us."

Jada shook her head. "Even in their early twenties, they seemed like grumpy old men. Brix and Press especially."

"Don't forget Zin Oliver. He's the grumpiest of them all."

She shuddered again. "Grumpy is being too nice. Zin is an asshole."

While, based on my interaction with Zin earlier today, I had to agree, the truth was the four of them were nothing like I'd always thought they were. Not that I knew them very well. The Avilas, Ridges, Barretts, and Olivers moved in different social circles than Jada and I did. Even though they were cousins, her family didn't have as much money as the Avilas.

"It always seems like Press has an English stick up his ass. Beau does too, just not as bad. They weren't even born there. They're as much American as we are."

"He's been really good to me," I said, wishing for the tenth or twentieth time since our call ended that I could talk to him again. "I feel so bad for him."

"It is sad. I remember when my dad died. That's still hard, and it's been a few years."

"Same here," I said. However, Jada had been a lot closer to her father than I'd been to mine. Especially since he'd spent the years before he died in a coma. "I remember thinking that was the absolute worst time of my life."

"I know. Kids at school were brutal."

Now, though, I knew life could get so much worse. I'd never been more terrified than I was in that shipping container after having been abducted by human traffickers. And now, to think there was a person, someone I didn't even know, who'd paid to have me kidnapped made me almost wretch. I shook my head, trying not to think about it, but how could I not? The same fear I'd felt then settled over me, suffocating me. I got off the bed and paced the room.

Jada sat up. "What's going on?"

"Panic attack," I said, trying to catch my breath.

"What can I do?"

I wanted to tell her to call Press. He, more than anyone, knew how to help me settle myself. "Seraphina," I said instead, sitting on the bed, hoping my heart rate would go down.

"Be right back." Jada raced out of the room and down the hallway to where my sister slept.

Seconds later, they both rushed in. Seraphina sat beside me, rubbing my back.

"Deep breaths," she said, reaching up to brush my hair from my face. "Jada, please go get a glass of water."

I rested my head on my sister's shoulder and closed my eyes, focusing on breathing in and out, slowing it with each breath I took.

"What brought this on?" she asked.

"Thinking. First about Dad. Then the container. Then that someone is out there who wants me taken again."

"Keep breathing," she repeated as she continued rubbing my back.

Jada returned to the room and handed me a glass of water. I took a sip, then held it out to her. I was about to lie down on the bed when I heard the cell phone Jacy had given me that morning ring.

"It's in the side pocket of my purse," I said to my sister, who was sitting close enough to reach it.

She looked at the screen. "It's Press. Do you want to talk to him?"

"I do," I said, holding out my hand for the phone. "Hi," I answered.

"Did I wake you?" he asked.

"Not at all. I'm sitting here with Seraphina and Jada."

"Oh, I won't keep you, then."

"Press? Wait."

"I'm still here."

"Can you hang on just a minute?"

When he said he could, I covered the phone with my hand. "Do you mind if I talk to him alone?" I asked.

"Of course not," my sister said, leading Jada out into the hallway.

"Sorry, I'm here. How are you, Press? How was today?"

"Long and exhausting. The boys left a few minutes ago. They're staying in the guesthouse you were in. Beau went with them, but Tryst is here. He and my dad are still downstairs, talking." He cleared his throat. "Don't let me keep you."

"You aren't. I want to talk to you. I, um, was in the midst of a panic attack when you called. Or coming out of one."

"Did something happen?"

"I let my mind wander."

"I'm so sorry I'm not there, Luisa."

I smiled. "Don't be. I'm a grown-up, right? I need to learn how to work through it on my own when it happens."

"Do you have a book you can read?"

"I think so. My tablet should be in my bag."

"Go and get it. I'll stay on the phone with you."

I knelt down and opened my suitcase. My tablet was right on top, but when I tried to power it on, nothing happened. "It's dead. I must've forgotten to charge it."

"I'm sure mine is here somewhere. Bear with me a moment."

"Press, you don't have to do this."

"I think tonight I need it as much as you do. Ah, here it is. Let's see now. Where were we?"

"Edward had just rescued Sophie from the evil Lord Ellington."

"Ah, yes. Here we are." He cleared his throat like he had earlier and began reading.

I drifted in and out of sleep while Press read. The main thing was the panic I'd felt dissipated, at least somewhat.

"You should get some sleep," I said.

"I shall. What about you? Will you be able to?"

"I feel a lot better. Thank you, Press." It was on the tip of my tongue to tell him how much I missed him, but like before, I couldn't bring myself to say it. While he'd become one of my closest friends and was so good to me, the time had to come when I stopped relying on him as much as I did.

I'd never heard him, or anyone else, mention a woman in his life. Not that I would've gotten wind of it. I hated to think he felt as though he had to hide something like that from me. Or that the amount of time he spent with me might cause problems in his relationship. Maybe that was why he'd disappeared before I left this morning. Maybe someone he was involved with had arrived at his parents' house. That didn't make sense, though. Why would he be talking to me now if he had another woman with him?

"Press?"

"Yes, pet?"

While I hadn't liked the term of endearment initially, it was growing on me. I knew he meant no disrespect by it. "Never mind."

"Get some rest. If you cannot sleep, ring me back, and we'll read some more."

"Why are you so good to me?"

"You make it easy to be. Good night, Luisa."

After ending our call, I got out of bed and went in search of Jada. I found her in the kitchen, talking to my mom and sister.

"How's Press doing?" Seraphina asked.

"You know Press."

She raised a brow.

"What I mean is he never worries about himself. Only others."

"I'm not sure 'others' is plural, sis. He worries about you."

I sat down at the table and took a sip when Jada handed me her glass of wine. "I was thinking about that earlier. I mean, what if he has a girlfriend?"

Seraphina laughed. "You can't be serious."

"Why not? Am I missing something here? Is Press gay?"

She shook her head. "Highly doubtful. There is one woman I know for certain he's very taken with."

I studied my sister. "If you mean me, it isn't that way between us. He's like an older brother to me."

She cocked her head. "Luisa…"

"You're wrong." I saw a look pass between my sister and mother, and it pissed me off. "I'm going to bed."

"I'll be up in a minute," said Jada when I handed the glass back to her.

When she came in, I faced the wall and feigned sleep. I didn't feel like talking any more tonight.

Actually, I did—to Press.

17

Press

This wasn't the type of book I'd read on my own, but I caught myself continuing to the end of the chapter anyway, smiling when I thought about Luisa's reaction if I told her I had. It was just one of the things she and I shared solely between us.

I set my tablet on the bedside table and stared up at the ceiling. "I wish you could've met her, Mum. She's amazing. Brave, strong, funny, gorgeous. She reminds me so much of you."

I closed my eyes, but quickly opened them, hating that the last time I'd seen her, she was kissing my brother.

"He doesn't love her the way I do. Father talked to me today and warned me against stepping to the side like I always do for him." I brushed a tear from my cheek. "I miss you, Mum. I hope you know how much Beau and I love you."

Rather than returning to the library of books on my tablet to look for something to read, I continued with the chapter after the one Luisa and I shared, adding a note to remind myself where she and I had left off.

My eyes drifted closed, and when they opened, the sunrise was visible through my window. After showering, I bundled up and took a walk in the vineyard. It had been a long time since I last had. At this time of year, the vines were dormant. I remembered taking a similar walk with my grandfather when I was a little boy.

"Let them sleep," he'd say. "They need their rest so, come springtime, they're ready to produce again."

Some of the vines still had leaves hanging. The colors varied greatly depending on the varietal, just like autumn leaves varied by tree species.

While being here made me nostalgic, I didn't regret the decision I'd made those years ago about not living here full-time like Beau did.

Overseeing the financial positions of the Barrett holdings was possible from Cambria, London, or anywhere else in the world I chose to be. I had no desire to commit to anything that would require me to remain at the property in Napa Valley, what we owned in Paso Robles, London, or anywhere else in the world.

As it had many times in the last few hours, my mind drifted to the kiss I'd witnessed between Beau and Luisa. How I longed to know the feel of her lips touching mine, her body nuzzled against me for more than "big brotherly" comfort. I wanted her to look at me the way she did at Beau—as a man she desired, a man she wanted. Was it foolish of me to think she ever would?

"Press!"

I spun around when I heard someone shout my name. Brix and Ridge were walking toward me.

"Good morning," I said when they joined me.

"You're out and about early," said Ridge, putting his hand on my shoulder. "How are you holding up?"

"I'm not certain it's hit me."

Brix nodded. "It took a long time for my father's death to catch up with me. I was so busy trying to bring in the harvest, I didn't have time to think or even to mourn him."

"Understood." I remembered that time well. Los Caballeros had stepped up to help with crush that year. However, the person who'd helped more than any other was Maddox Butler. When he and Alex Avila married, Ridge had believed his heart was broken. Then he'd met Seraphina. Their wedding, only a few days ago, was proof positive the two were meant to be together far more than Ridge was ever intended to be in a relationship with anyone else.

Was the same true for me? Was I pining for Luisa in the same way Ridge had been for Alex? Was I a fool to think there'd come a time she'd care for me the same way I did her? In the meantime, I wasn't getting any younger. Brix, Ridge, Zin, and I were considered the "old men" in Los Caballeros now. Along with Tryst. However, his role had become that of an advisor more than of a participating member. Not that he wasn't capable. The man was in better shape than I was.

"Shall we walk?" I asked, continuing on whether they followed or not.

"Listen, Ares asked about speaking with Luisa. Actually, what he wants is for her to talk with two profilers he's working with, Mayhem and Hanadarko," said Ridge as we wandered through rows of vines.

"I'm sure she'd agree to it if it would help find the person who's made her life a living hell," I said.

"Is it okay if I put her in touch with them directly?"

I stopped in my tracks. "Are you asking me?"

Ridge nodded.

"Why?"

His head cocked. "Because…"

Brix laughed.

I saw nothing humorous. "Since when am I Luisa's gatekeeper?"

Ridge didn't appear to find it any funnier than I did, based on the look he shot Brix. "Because you have been, Press. You can't deny it. Since shortly after we rescued her from that shipping container, you have tasked yourself with being the decision maker for anything to do with her."

"I have done, haven't I?" I said, continuing our walk. "My apologies."

"Hold up a minute," said Brix. "I may have been indisposed when all this went down, but wasn't her rescue something all the members of Los Caballeros agreed to help with?"

"Yes," answered Ridge. "We also agreed not to involve you at the time because you were going through your own stuff with Addy."

"I'm not suggesting you should've done otherwise. What I'm saying is Press is the one who needs us to step up since he's got his own family stuff going on. Can't someone else be the point person for Luisa? I'd be willing to do it."

"Perhaps the time has come for the woman to be her own point person." I stared off in the distance rather than make eye contact with two of the men most likely to recognize my pain. I'd taken on that job without anyone asking me to—Luisa included. It wouldn't be easy for me to let it go.

"Okay, but even Seraphina suggested I talk to you about it first," said Ridge.

"Very well, I'll speak with Luisa."

"Press, what's going on? Is there something more besides your mom? I know that's enough, but even before that, at our wedding, you seemed distracted."

"You said it yourself. I tasked *myself* with being the middleman with anything to do with Luisa. I had no right."

"It's what happened with Beau, isn't it?" asked Zin, who I hadn't seen approach.

"What happened with Beau?" Brix asked.

"He kissed her," Zin responded.

"Bloody hell," I muttered, stalking away in the direction of the main house. Like the one I had with my dad, this was not a conversation I wanted any part of. It was hard enough to see it replay in my mind again and again; I didn't need to *talk* about it.

I could hear my three friends on my heels and picked up my pace. Any faster and I'd break into a run. Instead, I came to a sudden stop and spoke without turning to look at them. "As I said, I will speak with Luisa regarding this final request. However, after I do, please address her directly."

"Let me handle it, Press," said Brix.

"Right. Good. You handle it." This time when I stormed off, they went in the opposite direction.

The following day, we stood in the family cemetery on the grounds of the Barrett Estate and laid my mother's ashes to rest.

Beau, my father, and I were surrounded by our closest friends. Ones who were like family to us. Ridge's father, Hewitt, had flown in, as had Zin's father,

Michael. They stood alongside my dad and Tryst, who spoke a few words before inviting my brother and me to do so. Neither of us did.

I couldn't attest to how Beau felt, but I'd spoken with my mother many times in the days since she passed. There was nothing I needed or wanted to say publicly.

Part of me wished Luisa was here too. However, that she'd be here to comfort Beau more than me caused the ache in my chest over the loss of my mother to worsen.

I hadn't spoken with her since I last read a few chapters of our book to her. Brix had offered to talk with her about Ares' request, and she hadn't reached out to me about it or anything else. Thus, I hadn't contacted her either.

We returned to the main residence, and I excused myself from the group. Once I reached the bedroom, I realized the thing I wanted to do most—speak with Luisa—was the last thing I should do. The sooner I weaned myself from her, the better.

I changed out of the suit I wore to the graveside and returned downstairs, appreciating that we'd decided to keep today private. I doubted my brother or father could've withstood a parade of people through the house again today any better than I could.

"Have you thought about how long you'll stay?" Brix asked, approaching when I poured myself a glass of wine.

"At least a few days. Beyond that, I've no idea." Before making any decisions, I'd need to talk it over with Beau, who must've excused himself like I had.

I itched to ask Brix if everything had been arranged for Luisa's call with the profilers. I refrained, though, reminding myself again it was for the best if I removed myself from being her self-appointed guardian.

"You needn't stick around," I said, realizing it might be the reason he'd asked about my intentions.

"Ridge and I will head home in the morning, unless there's something more we can do."

"I appreciate it. That you were here at all meant a great deal to me."

"Of course we would be. We're brothers," he said, gripping my shoulder.

"Have you seen Beau?" my dad asked a few minutes later.

"I've not." I was about to offer to check on him, but thought better of it when it occurred to me he may be talking to Luisa. "He likely just needs a few minutes on his own."

My father nodded and walked away.

When my brother hadn't reappeared an hour later, I went looking. Beau lived in a separate residence on the estate but had spent the last two nights in the bedroom adjacent to mine. The two rooms were separated by a shared bathroom as well as two walk-in closets. When I didn't find him anywhere upstairs, it occurred to me he may have gone back to his place.

"Have you seen Beau?" I asked Cru Avila, my brother's closest friend, when I returned downstairs.

"He left. Didn't he tell you?"

"Left? Back to his place?"

Cru shook his head. "He said he was flying out. When he didn't say where, I didn't ask. I figured you knew, though."

"I didn't, and I doubt my father did either since, a little over an hour ago, he asked if I'd seen him."

Cru checked his watch. "It's been close to two hours since he left."

"Thanks."

What in the bloody hell was my brother up to? I walked out of the room and rang him, but it went straight to voicemail. My father met me in the hall.

"Were you aware Beau was leaving?" I asked.

"Leaving?"

"That was my response when Cru told me he's been gone over two hours. Apparently, he told him he was flying out."

When my father merely nodded but didn't comment, a feeling of dread settled over me. Was he on his way to see Luisa? Was that why I hadn't heard from her? I'd know soon enough if I mentioned it to Ridge.

18

Luisa

"Have you talked to Ridge?" I asked my sister.

"Yes, a few minutes ago. Why?"

"Did he say how Press and Beau are doing?"

"Actually, he asked me if you'd heard from Beau."

"I haven't heard from either of them." It seemed odd that she'd ask about Beau specifically. I was more concerned I hadn't spoken to his brother.

"Ridge said Beau left. He was catching a flight somewhere. He thought he might be on his way here."

"Why here?"

Seraphina shrugged, and my eyes met Jada's. She motioned with her head, and I followed her into another room.

"What about the kiss?" she whispered.

"I doubt that means he's coming here."

"Jacy would know, right?" said Jada.

I shrugged like my sister had.

"Let's ask her."

We found her talking with Tank; both were standing right outside the front door.

"Is everything okay?" she asked when we joined them.

"Did Beau Barrett contact you about coming here?"

"He has not. Do you have reason to believe he might be?" Jacy asked.

"Ridge asked my sister if we'd heard from him."

"I haven't." Jacy looked at Tank. "Have you?"

"Negative, and if he'd contacted one of the other guys, they would've informed Jacy or me."

"We'll be on the lookout, given the circumstances, but he's been briefed that no one comes or goes without alerting us."

"Thanks, Jacy."

"If you do speak with him and he's planning to come to the ranch, please let me know right away," she said when Jada and I turned to go inside.

"Is it me, or does this seem weird?" I asked.

Jada shrugged. "I'm not the right person to ask."

"Why not?"

"I think all those guys are weird."

I smiled. In a way, I agreed. Since I'd gotten to know most of them, though, they didn't seem as odd to me now.

"When's the last time you talked to Press?" she asked.

"The night before last."

"Maybe you should call him."

"I don't want to bug him. He usually checks in with me."

When another day passed without any word from him, I was tempted. Instead, when Ridge arrived to pick Seraphina up, I asked about him.

"Press is doing okay. Beau taking off is irritating, but it isn't that unlike him."

"No one knows where he went?" I asked.

"I have my suspicions."

"Where?"

Ridge sighed. "My guess is he went to Australia to see Daphne."

Two days after he kissed me. That should irk me more than it did. "I'm surprised she didn't come to the funeral."

"There wasn't a lot of time. Plus, the Barretts requested the graveside service be private. Maybe that's why she didn't," said Ridge.

"Do you know when Press is coming back?"

Ridge looked from me to my sister.

"What?" I asked.

"He's staying in Napa indefinitely," he responded.

"What about Seahorse?"

When Ridge studied me, I wondered if the panic I felt was evident in the tone of my voice.

"He's left it for extended periods of time in the past," he said.

"What's wrong, Luisa?" my sister asked.

"Nothing." I went upstairs, into the bedroom, and closed the door behind me before my first tear fell. Press was staying in Napa indefinitely and hadn't even called or texted to tell me? Maybe he didn't think it was any of my business. But we usually talked every day. At least once. In fact, this was the longest we'd gone without seeing each other since I'd been rescued from the shipping container.

The door opened, and Jada came in. "You should call him."

"Who? Beau or Press?"

"Press."

"If he wants to talk to me, he knows the number."

Jada shook her head. "Instead of just picking up the phone yourself, you'll hide out in the bedroom and cry. You're so stubborn."

"He obviously has more important things to take care of." More important than taking care of me, I thought but didn't say. He'd spent the last two months worrying about me and only me. It was time to let him off the hook and manage on my own.

"Luisa, Press cares about you. Everyone knows it."

I lay on the bed and looked up at the ceiling the same way I had the last time Jada and I talked about Press. "Maybe he thinks it's time I learned to take care of myself. I don't disagree."

"Maybe he isn't calling you because you're not calling him."

"I doubt it."

"Argh," I heard her growl before she left the room.

I pulled out my phone and, before I could talk myself out of it, sent him a text. *I'm thinking about you. Hope you're doing okay.*

I waited, but there was no sign he was responding. When an hour passed and he still hadn't, I put my head in the pillow and cried harder.

"What?" I barked when there was a knock at the door.

"Hey," said Seraphina, coming over to sit beside me on the bed.

"I'm fine. Okay?"

"I can tell."

I looked over my shoulder at her, and she smiled.

"What's up?" I asked.

"Was Brix able to talk to you about the two profilers investigating your case wanting to interview you?"

I felt my body stiffen and rolled my shoulders. "No."

"Would you be willing to?"

I shrugged, wishing so much I could talk to Press about it. I pulled out my phone and checked, hoping he'd replied. He hadn't. "I guess I should."

"As for Press, his mother died; I'm sure that's—"

"I can't believe you said that. Do you think I forgot? I'm not that self-centered."

"That isn't what I meant. I was trying to make you feel better."

I rolled onto my back. "I know and I'm sorry. I hadn't realized how dependent I am on him." I bit my lip, which did nothing to quell my tears.

"Have you tried contacting him?" she asked.

I nodded.

"I'm sorry, sweetie. And I know I upset you when I said this before, but he probably has a lot going on."

"I know." I covered my face with my hands. "I just…I can't believe I'm saying this, but…I miss him."

"What about Beau?"

"What do you mean?"

"You were pretty upset when you found out he had a girlfriend."

I was still mortified whenever I thought about the way I'd acted that day. It was childish. Almost as childish as I was behaving now. "Press is different. Besides you and Jada, he's my best friend."

When tears flooded my eyes once again, my sister pulled me into her arms. "Tell him that."

"How can I when he isn't talking to me?"

She pulled back and looked into my eyes. "Grant him some grace."

I nodded. She was right. I'd gotten used to him responding right away. Now, he had more important matters to attend to.

"Come on, let's go find Ridge and let him know you're ready to talk to the profilers."

I got up to follow and left my phone where it was on the bed. If I brought it with me, I'd keep checking every two minutes to see if Press had responded. Like a teenager.

Since it was midnight in London, where the profilers were, Ridge, Seraphina, Jada, and I walked over to the main house. Laird was sitting on the front porch, smoking a pipe.

"Sorcha is inside," he said, looking directly at me. "She'll be happy to see you."

I wanted to ask why, but that would've made me sound even more like a kid.

"There you are, lass," she said when we walked in the front door. Even though she'd shouted it, she put her finger in front of her lips and looked down at the little boy asleep in her arms.

"We'll come back later," whispered Seraphina.

"That's okay. I've got him," said Bradley, coming out of the kitchen and taking the boy out of his grandmother's arms.

"I hear there are people in London who would like to speak with you," Sorcha said to me, holding out her hand so I'd sit beside her.

"I've decided you receive a report on the world's happenings every morning," Ridge said, chuckling.

Sorcha raised a brow. "You would be correct."

He laughed out loud. "I'm not surprised."

She turned to me. "Do you have any questions before you speak with them?"

"I don't think so. Should I?"

"I'll be with you, so if you do, then, we'll ask."

While I hadn't expected her to be, that she would when Press couldn't was reassuring.

"I won't be talking to them until tomorrow morning."

"Aye, lass. The call is scheduled for zero eight hundred."

"How am I not surprised you know that before I do?"

Sorcha patted my hand. "You're catching on, my dear." She looked over at Ridge. "Don't you have a honeymoon planned for your bride?"

"Of course, he does," Seraphina answered. "We're waiting until things calm down a little."

"You can stay for dinner, but afterward, the two of you need to be on your way. Bradley and I have this covered. If we need help, Jada is here."

"You don't have to stick around, you know," I leaned over and whispered to my friend.

"What if I want to?"

"She'll be stayin'," said Sorcha, winking at Jada and me.

"I guess you're stuck here, then," I teased.

The change in expression on her face jarred me. Jada was the joker between the two of us. "Is there something you know I don't?" I whispered.

Her eyes filled with tears.

"*What?* Tell me!"

"I can't bear the idea of coming so close to losing you again."

"You aren't going to." I pointed to Zeppelin, who I could see outside with Magnet. "I mean, just look at those two."

Jada leaned closer. "Believe me, I have been looking."

19

Press

To say I was livid with my brother was putting it mildly. If it wouldn't mean leaving my father on his own, I'd fly to Australia and drag his arse home. Not that I was certain he was headed there. After Paso Robles, to see Luisa, which I was assured wasn't the case, it was the best guess.

"It's our slow time of the year," said my father. "He's taking advantage of it."

"Would've been nice of him to inform us, at the very least."

"You know your brother."

If the words hadn't been uttered in baritone, I would've expected them to come from my mother. I'd heard her say the same thing so often.

"When will we cease excusing his behavior?" I spat.

"When it's necessary to do so. Now, it's not."

"Sorry."

He nodded. "You don't need to stay either, Lavery. I'm perfectly capable of managing on my own."

"It will soon be time to prune the vines."

"I can oversee it," he insisted.

"You shouldn't have to. That's Beau's job, as is prepping for bottling."

"I can handle that as well."

"What about wine club shipments and calculating restaurant allocation in the coming year?"

My father raised a brow, which irritated me as much as my brother's swift departure had. Just because I focused more on the financial management of our business, it didn't mean I was unaware of the day-to-day operations.

"I'll hire as much help as I need."

"I'm not leaving, Dad. Nothing you say will change my mind."

He nodded, apparently resigned to my decision. "What about Luisa?"

"It was probably an error in judgment, bringing her here in the first place. My apologies for not consulting with you about it prior to doing so."

"We would've welcomed her gladly, you know that."

We. My father wasn't part of a "we" anymore. I wondered if his status as a widower had sunk in yet. Likely not. Grief came in stages, and it was early in the mourning process for all three of us.

"She's safer where she is."

"I take it you have no recollection of our conversation."

"No, I do, and I appreciate your meddling very much."

My father laughed.

"Truly, though, what's between Luisa and me is complicated. Or rather, completely uncomplicated, given it's nothing."

"You may be able to lie to yourself about it, but you've never been successful doing so with your mother and me."

I stopped myself from wincing at his mention of the two of them collectively. However, he didn't seem at all fazed by it. Perhaps I was overthinking. They'd had been a team since long before I came along. It wouldn't be easy or swift for my dad to think of them any other way.

"I haven't heard from her since the day she left. Or that night, rather. Either way, it's time she stood on her own two feet without my interference."

"Would she agree?" he asked.

"Her lack of communication is indicative of it."

"Or she doesn't want to intrude."

"It hasn't stopped her in the past." I smiled at the recollection. Her behavior at the wedding alone, prior to finding out she remained in danger, suggested she was growing more comfortable speaking her mind. Not that it was the same as being intrusive. "Perhaps I'll ring her later."

My dad stood and walked out of the room, heading in the direction of his study. "No time like the present," he shouted behind him.

"I suppose he's right," I muttered to myself, realizing I'd left my mobile upstairs, something that was completely unlike me to do.

When I retrieved it from the table where I'd been sitting earlier, I saw a text notification. *I'm thinking about you. Hope you're doing okay,* the message from Luisa read. I was stunned to see it was sent two hours ago.

Rather than send a text response, I rang her, disappointed when the call went to voicemail. "Thanks for your message. We're hanging in," I said, ending the call before I could tell her I missed her with every fiber of my being. I even thought about calling back just to hear her voice again.

I opened the laptop I'd also left on the table and sifted through my overflowing email inbox, glancing every so often to see if Luisa had sent another message as well as checking—more than once—to make sure I'd turned the volume up high enough that if she rang, I'd hear it.

While in the midst of reading the email Ares had sent two days ago about arranging for a call between Luisa and the two profilers he was working with, my mobile rang. I grabbed it, elated to see it was the woman herself calling.

"Hello," I answered. "How are you?"

"I'm okay, Press. How are you?"

"As well as can be expected, I suppose."

"I hope I'm not bothering you."

I sat back in my chair, closed my eyes, and pictured the look on her face. "Don't bite your lip," I muttered out of habit.

She laughed, and it was the most joyous sound. "How did you know?"

"I know you," I said softly.

"Press, I…"

"Go on."

"You've got a lot going on there. I don't want to bother you."

"That's the second time you've said something to that effect, and you're not. You never do," I insisted.

"You'd never admit it even if I did."

I smiled. "How are things at Butler Ranch? I trust Sorcha is keeping you well-fed."

"She's doing her best. I…um…Ridge said you were staying in Napa indefinitely."

"I'm sure he also informed you my brother has fled the coop, so to speak."

"Where is he?"

I hated to tell her my theory, given I knew hearing Daphne's name would likely upset her.

"Australia?" she asked before I could respond.

"I believe so."

"It makes sense. I'm sure he's devastated about your mom and would want to be with Daphne."

I was stunned by her casual tone. I didn't pick up on the slightest hint of jealousy.

"What about you, Press? How are you coping?"

Not anywhere near as well as I would be if I could simply hold Luisa's hand and feel her beside me.

"Press?"

"I'm here."

"I should probably let you go."

No, no, not yet, I wanted to shout. "So soon?"

"You seem distracted."

"Not at all. I'm entirely devoted to talking with you. How've you been? No panic attacks, I trust?"

"Jada is still here. That helps," she told me.

"I'm glad."

"Okay, well, um…"

"Tell me what's on your mind, pet." I cringed. She hated when I used what I considered a term of endearment. "Sorry. *Luisa,*" I emphasized her name.

"It's okay. It doesn't bother me when you call me that."

"Since when? I distinctly remember your scowl and reprimand when I did it at the wedding. That wasn't so long ago."

"It feels like forever."

It did to me as well. Every minute away from her felt like a lifetime. Best to rip the bandage off now, though. At least I'd be preoccupied with the work to be done here. *Ha!* Who was I kidding? Nothing would stop me from thinking about her.

"Is that funny?"

Good God, had I laughed out loud? "No, no, of course not."

"Why did you chuckle?"

"It had nothing to do with you saying the wedding feels like forever ago."

I heard her sigh.

"Luisa…"

"Yes?"

I'd probably regret my words, but I had to say them. "I miss you."

"Oh, thank God," she said, audibly letting out the breath she'd been holding. "I miss you too."

"I've wanted to call."

"Why didn't you?"

Why hadn't I? What misguided advice had I been giving myself? Ah, I remembered. "I thought it best to give you space."

"I told you at the wedding that if I wanted space, I'd say so."

"You didn't contact me either, pet."

"I was giving you space."

I laughed. "Touché."

"There's something we need to talk about," she began.

"I'm listening."

"The kiss."

The two words were akin to her stabbing me in the heart. "Yes, the kiss."

"I didn't expect Beau to do that."

"And yet he did."

"I know you won't believe me, but I didn't want him to."

She was right. I found it hard to believe. "What makes you say so?" I asked anyway.

"I know it seemed like I had a crush on him."

I murmured my agreement.

"I'm over it."

"So easily? Does it have anything to do with the possibility he's in Australia?"

"Press."

"Luisa."

"I'm not interested in Beau, okay? I mean, I'm not interested in anyone. How could I be? There's some lunatic out there who wants to *buy* me, for God's sake."

Not…interested…in…anyone. Those words hurt just as much as the reminder of the kiss. And she was right. How could she be? "I hate to cut this short, but I've a meeting starting in a few minutes I'm not entirely prepared for. Perhaps we can talk again later?"

"Of course. Right. *My apologies.*" The last bit was said mimicking the words I said so often. "Bye, Press."

She ended the call without my having the chance to say anything else. It was probably for the best, given I doubted I could mask the disappointment

I felt. *Unjustly* felt. Luisa had never hidden the fact that I wasn't someone she was interested in. While the confirmation didn't come as a surprise, it didn't stop it from hurting.

The minute I set my mobile down, I regretted lying and saying I had a meeting. Besides the conversations between my father and me, I had no plans to speak with anyone in the near future. If I hadn't reacted so hastily, I would still be enjoying the pleasure of her voice, her wit, her everything.

My mobile rang again, and since I knew it wouldn't be Luisa, I thought about not even picking it up. However, if it was Beau calling, I'd hate to miss the opportunity to give him a piece of my mind. Instead, I saw it was Zin.

"Hello, counselor."

"How goes it?" he asked.

"Not a lot differently than before you departed earlier. My father is encouraging me to abandon him like my brother has, which I refuse to do."

"Seraphina is worried about her sister."

"We all are, and frankly, I'm surprised this news is coming through you."

"She thought you'd listen to me."

"How misguided of her."

Zin laughed. "That's what I said."

"You took it upon yourself to call anyway."

"I know I've been an asshole about it, but the two of you look equally miserable. Before you say it, I am aware your mother died, Press. Still, your entire demeanor changed once the SUV transporting Luisa to Butler Ranch pulled away."

There was nothing for me to dispute. He was right. I felt like a part of me left with her. And perhaps it had.

"I spoke with her a few minutes ago."

"I'm aware," he said.

"How?"

"She came downstairs after your call ended."

"And?"

"It was evident she'd been crying."

I groaned inwardly. "I doubt it had anything to do with me."

"You should be very happy I'm not in Napa right now, Press."

"Why is that?"

"I'd give you the punch in the face you so richly deserve for being a complete idiot about this."

Zin and I sparred regularly as part of our workout routine. "You'd never land one."

He sighed. "I have an idea. Actually, it was Seraphina's idea, but she wasn't sure about the logistics of it."

Logistics? I was intrigued. "Go on."

"Given we're beyond Christmas, we're entering the slowest time of the year for the wine business. The tasting rooms aren't on the property anyway, so even if they were busy, it wouldn't matter."

"Your point?"

"You know Ridge was talking about hiring Luisa, right?"

I was ready to reach through the phone and throttle him. "Point, Zin?"

"Why don't you hire her? She can help with the stuff you normally do, so you can help your dad with the stuff Beau normally does."

"Hold up a minute. Have you talked to him?"

"I have," he admitted.

Bloody hell. "He called you and not our father? Or me? How long does he intend to be away?"

"He doesn't know."

"Selfish *sonuvabitch*. I hope to hell Noah Cullen knocks some sense into the bastard." The man had been a member of Los Caballeros at the same time my father, Ridge's, and Zin's had been. Brix's father had led the group back then, the same way Brix did now. The Cullens were like family, which made the relationship between Beau and Daphne all the more complicated.

"He isn't going to Australia."

"Where's he going?"

Zin cleared his throat. "He wouldn't say."

"This is preposterous. He knows we have the ability to track him."

"Maybe so, Press, but he begged me to convince you this is the right thing for him."

Something else occurred to me. "My father already knows this, doesn't he?"

"He's aware."

"Meaning he spoke with my brother?"

"Yes, Press."

"I'll ring you back." As much as I wanted to hurl the phone against the wall, I set it on the table and went in search of my dad.

20

Luisa

"Press will never agree to it, and besides, he's got so much going on. I can't be an added burden."

"Zin is talking to him now, and that Press has so much going on is the point, Luisa. He needs the help, and you have the ability and the education to provide it. Think of it as giving back some of what he's given you."

"So I'd work for Barrett Family Vintners for free?"

My sister cocked her head. "No one is suggesting you work for free, Luisa."

"I wouldn't feel right accepting money from them."

I looked up when Ridge walked into the room. "I heard the Barretts are hiring you away from us," he said, winking.

"Nothing has been decided. Besides, you never actually offered me a job."

"He was going to. I asked him to wait," said Seraphina.

I folded my arms. "Why?"

"For a lot of reasons. First and foremost, you were still staying here at Butler Ranch. Not to mention I needed your help with the wedding."

"What about Mom? Where will she go? I mean, if Press even agrees to this."

"Mom is going to live with us." She lowered her voice. "By the way, we didn't tell Mom about…you know, you."

"Wait. Are you serious?" I looked between my sister and her husband.

"About which part?" Seraphina whispered.

"Mom living with you."

"Yes," Ridge responded.

"We hadn't necessarily planned for her to move in right away, but a few months from now, definitely."

"Mom agreed?"

"Yes, Luisa," I heard her shout from the other room. "They'll need my help with my new grandbaby."

Seraphina groaned. "Thanks, Mom. Way to spoil the surprise."

I jumped up and hugged my sister. "You're pregnant? Oh my God, I'm so happy for you." I hugged Ridge too. "This is wonderful." I felt my eyes fill with tears. It was nice to be crying over something happy, for a change.

"It's one of the reasons we postponed the honeymoon. I'm not feeling well enough to travel much presently."

"Why didn't you say something sooner?" I asked.

Ridge's phone vibrated, and he excused himself.

"We wanted to keep it between the two of us for a while. When the time comes you and the man you love find out you're having a baby together, I'm sure you'll feel the same way we did."

I didn't see that happening for me, but I wouldn't be a Debbie Downer and spoil my sister's happiness.

Zin came inside. "Where's Ridge?" he stuck his head in the kitchen and asked.

"I'm not sure. He got a phone call and left," Seraphina told him.

He nodded and went out the way he'd come in.

"See? Press must've said no."

My sister shook her head. "Something else is going on. I think it's about Beau."

"Is he in Australia?" I asked.

"I don't believe so."

"Hmm."

"Yes, that about sums it up."

I was headed upstairs to look for her when Jada came down. "I'm going home for a bit. I can come back later tonight, though."

I hugged her. "You don't have to. I'm okay, I promise. Plus, my mom and sister are here. And if I'm feeling really low, I'll just pay Sorcha a visit. At the very least, she'll feed me."

She laughed, but the smile left her face when Zin followed Ridge through the front door.

"You're leaving?" he asked, looking at her bag.

"Yes."

"What was that about?" I whispered when the two men went into the kitchen.

"Ugh. I can't stand him."

"I didn't realize you knew him well enough to care one way or another."

She shrugged, and even though we couldn't see him or Ridge any longer, she stuck her tongue out in that direction.

"Okay, there's a story here."

"Not a very interesting one." She leaned forward and kissed my cheek. "I'll see you later. Call me when he's gone, and I'll come back."

"I already told you I'll be fine."

"Call me anyway."

She wasn't out the door more than a minute when Zin returned. "Did Jada leave?"

"She told you she was going to. What's the deal with you two?"

"Why? What did she say?"

"She told me everything."

Zin's face paled.

"I'm kidding! Oh my God. Now, I really want to know."

"There's nothing to tell."

"Right. That's why when I said she told me every-thing, you looked like you swallowed a turd."

His nose scrunched. "Ew. Don't say shit like that." He winked and walked out the front door.

"Ha, ha. I'm going to pester both of you until one of you tells me," I shouted after him.

It was only when I saw his car pulling away from the house that I remembered he hadn't said anything about his conversation with Press.

I pulled my phone out of my pocket, wishing there was a message from him, even though I knew better than to expect one. We'd gone from talking at least once a day—usually so he could tell me when he planned to stop by Butler Ranch, where we'd talk for hours—to one ten-minute, uber-awkward conversation.

I sighed and sat beside my mother on the living room sofa. "So you're moving in with Ridge and Seraphina?"

"I'll have my own quarters."

I raised a brow.

"Ridge called it a mother-in-law suite. He said I'd have plenty of privacy. He showed me photos, and it looks bigger than our whole apartment."

It wouldn't surprise me if she was right. The Ridge family was very wealthy, as were the Barretts. We could've fit five of our apartments in the "guesthouse" I'd stayed in.

"I'm happy for you, Mom."

"I was so sorry to hear Press' mother passed away."

"It's very sad," I agreed.

"I'm surprised you're here instead of with him."

"They kept it private."

My mother raised a brow.

"What?"

"Press rarely leaves your side, and when he does, he comes back the following morning."

"We're friends. I would've just been in the way."

"It's Beau, isn't it? I wish you would wake up and realize he's not the man for you."

"I have."

My mother *clapped* her hands.

"Are you kidding me right now?"

"Finally," she said, squeezing my cheeks with one hand. "Press is so much better for you."

"Whoa, whoa, whoa! I said I realized Beau is not the man for me. I didn't say anything about Press."

She rolled her eyes. "What else do you expect the man to do, Luisa? He would lay the world at your feet if you asked."

"He cares about me, Mom, but there's nothing romantic between us."

"You're a very smart girl, but sometimes I think part of your brain goes to sleep."

"What does that mean?"

"Press is in love with you, my darling daughter. It's time you woke up and realized it."

I looked down at my phone and saw a message alert.

"It's him, isn't it?" my mother asked, leaning over to see the screen.

"I don't know who it's from."

"Well, look!"

I stood, walked over to the staircase, and swiped the screen. I saw the name Barrett. However, the message wasn't from Press; it was from Beau.

I just want you to know I'm sorry.

Call me, I responded.

When my phone rang seconds later, I raced up the steps and into the bedroom so I could talk to him without anyone eavesdropping.

"Hi."

"Hello. I guess you got my text," he said.

"I did."

"Again, I want you to know how sorry I am."

"Beau, what is this about? There's nothing for you to be sorry for."

"Luisa." It was one word. My name. But the anguish in his voice said so much more. "I shouldn't have kissed you like I did."

I expected his words to hurt, but they didn't. "Apology accepted."

"I'll be in touch. Bye, Luisa."

I looked at the screen when I heard the chimes indicating the call ended, once again anticipating the hurt I'd felt in the past when Beau acted disinterested, but I felt nothing.

My sister was still in the kitchen, sitting at the table with Ridge, when I returned downstairs.

"Is everything okay?" she asked.

I shook my head. "I just talked to Beau."

Ridge's eyes opened wide. "He contacted you?"

"First he texted, then called."

Ridge reached over to take my sister's hand. "Sera, I need to talk to Zin."

She nodded. "Do whatever you need to do, Noah."

When we were growing up, my sister hated being referred to as Sera, and from what I knew, no one called

Noah anything but Ridge. It made me think about Press calling me "pet." When he did, it didn't bother me. If anyone else attempted to, I would bristle.

"I feel bad for Beau. From what Ridge has said, he and his mother were very close," Seraphina commented.

"Press was close to her too." I wished it had been him who called rather than his brother just so I could tell him how sorry I was and comfort him like he'd always done for me.

"From now on, Christmas will be an especially difficult day for them," she said.

So much had happened in those twenty-four hours. Ridge and Seraphina's wedding. Me finding out someone had offered money to have me abducted. Traveling from Mexico to Napa Valley, then arriving at Press' parents' home and learning his mother had been taken to the hospital by helicopter and had passed away.

"Do you think I should tell Press about my phone call with his brother?"

Seraphina tapped her bottom lip with the tip of her index finger. "I'm not sure. I mean, all he really did was apologize for kissing you."

"I told Press I missed him."

While it had taken courage for me to say the words to Press, it was made easier because he said them first. My confession didn't appear to register with my sister.

"Did you hear me?" I asked.

Her eyes met mine. "Yes."

"It was a big deal for me to say it."

Seraphina smiled. "I couldn't love you more than I do, Luisa, but you and Press…"

"What about us?"

"I've never seen two people less aware."

I folded my arms and rested against the chair. "Explain, please."

She rolled her eyes. "As soon as you pull your head out of the sand, you'll see it for yourself."

When she got up and left the kitchen, I didn't follow.

21

Press

"You've spoken with Beau," I said, finding my dad in his study, sitting behind his desk.

"Yes."

"Why didn't you say?"

"I knew you'd ask questions for which I had no answers."

"Where is he?"

"Nowhere in particular."

I took a seat. "This is tedious, Father, even for you."

When he winced, I regretted my words as much as my tone. "We all process grief in our own way, son."

"He has responsibilities."

My father sighed. "As I said before, I can handle them. Honestly, Lavery, staying busy will help me cope as well."

I understood, recalling I'd thought as much about Luisa. That staying busy would keep me from thinking about how much I missed her. I doubted it would, in the same way I doubted my father would think of my mother any less.

"Why didn't he tell me?"

My father raised a brow and cocked his head. "Do you really need to ask?"

I'd go on about how unfair my brother's actions were, but it would only result in my dad insisting he didn't need me to stay on in Napa. "Did he take the plane?" I asked instead. The question was ridiculous. He could hardly fly it solo.

"He did not."

"Zin suggested I bring Luisa on to help with things here. She has an MBA and could assist with many of the daily tasks related to the financial management of our family's holdings."

My father nodded.

"You're already aware of this as well?" While my frustration over my brother's actions had dissipated slightly, the idea that other conversations were taking place, essentially circumventing me, made me angry.

"No one has spoken with me about this, Lavery. I was merely nodding to indicate I was listening."

"My apologies," I muttered under my breath.

"Tell me your concerns."

"You did say you were aware she's facing an imminent threat. If we agree to hire her, bring her here, it would necessitate additional security."

"I've always left that to you anyway. Back when my parents lived here, we never even locked the door."

I'd set the estate as well as the London property up with the best security available. Even then, I wouldn't want to bring Luisa back here without the detail team K19 had arranged for her to have.

"You seem happier already," said my father, studying me.

"I'm hardly happy, Dad."

"This woman soothes your soul. It's evident."

He was right; she did, but was that fair to her? She'd said, in no uncertain terms, that she wasn't interested in anyone romantically. That included me. If she agreed to work for Barrett Family Enterprises, agreed to return to Napa Valley, it would be on a professional and platonic basis only.

Rather than returning Zin's call after my conversation with my father ended, I rang Luisa directly.

"Hi," she said, answering once more before I'd even heard it connect on her end.

"Hello."

"I was hoping I'd hear from you again."

"My apologies for cutting our conversation short earlier."

"How was your meeting?"

"There wasn't one," I confessed.

I could hear background noise, so I knew she was still on the line. However, she didn't speak.

"I find myself unsettled, Luisa. Part of it is my mum, of course, but after spending the last several weeks seeing you most every day and talking to you when I didn't, it feels as though something is missing. Not something. Someone. You."

"I feel the same way." Her voice sounded as tentative as I felt while sharing what I'd previously held close.

"I trust Zin has spoken with you about working for our family business?"

"He has. I don't want you to feel obligated to hire me, though."

"It seems my brother is taking an extended leave of absence, meaning I will be responsible for more of his duties. Zin suggested you would be an ideal fit to assist with the overflow of what I'm unable to manage.

It will consist primarily of financial report preparation and monitoring assets and liabilities. Things of that nature."

"If I can help, I'd like to."

"It would be much appreciated. How soon can you start?" I asked.

"When would you like me to?"

I chuckled. "Would tomorrow be too soon?"

"I can't tell if you're serious or joking, but no, tomorrow would not be too soon."

My heart felt infinitely lighter, knowing that sometime in the next twenty-four hours, I'd look into her eyes and see her smile.

"I'd come tonight if I could," she said quietly enough I wasn't certain I'd heard her correctly.

"Why is that, pet?" I ventured.

"I'm supposed to talk to the profilers in the morning."

"There's no reason for you to leave prior to doing so."

She sighed. "That isn't what I meant. Or not what I'm worried about. I'd much rather wait until you can be with me."

"If you're serious, I can make arrangements."

"It's too much to ask."

I smiled, picturing her. "Stop biting your lip, pet."

She laughed. "Yes, Press."

"If you really want to come to Napa tonight, I can make it happen."

"You know what? No. I can handle this conversation on my own. It's not like I have to talk to Jorge, or whatever his real name is. I'm not even sure why they want to talk to me. While I appreciate your willingness to take care of me like you always do, you don't have to."

Admittedly, I was disappointed, but she was right. It would be an extravagance and no easy feat to bring her up here tonight. It would mean finding someone to fly the Cessna with me, then immediately making the return trip. "If you're sure."

"I am, but can we talk again later? There's something else I want to talk to you about."

"We can do that now if you'd like."

"I'd rather wait."

"No problem. Perhaps we can also pick up where we left off in our book."

She sighed. "I'd love to."

After ending the call, I went in search of my father, who I found in the same place I'd left him.

"What would you say about a quick trip to Seahorse tomorrow?"

He rested against his chair and removed his glasses. "It sounds ideal. Will we be making any other stops? Say to Butler Ranch?" He winked. "I'd love to see Laird and Sorcha."

"That can be arranged."

"Must we wait until tomorrow? It's a quick flight." There was a twinkle in my father's eyes that warmed my heart. If his meddling in my "relationship" with Luisa took away his sadness for only a few moments, I was glad.

After speaking with Jaicon, I rang Sorcha, requesting she allow me to surprise Luisa.

"Aye, it will be a delight to see her face light up when you arrive." She asked if I thought my father would mind if she also invited Tryst Avila, Hewitt Ridge, and Michael Oliver over as well.

"My father would be delighted to spend more time with good friends," I assured her.

"Thank you, son," my dad said when he got in the passenger side of the Range Rover we'd leave at the Napa private airfield until we returned. "A change of scenery will do me good."

"We can stay as long as you'd like," I told him, eyeing the size of the bag he tossed in the back.

"It will be at least two weeks before we can begin pruning the vines."

"Sounds good to me."

The drive from my parents' place to the airfield took longer than it would to fly and land at Seahorse.

Beau and I had talked about building a landing strip on the Napa property a few years ago, like what I had at my place. However, the bureaucracy involved in getting it done made it prohibitive. If I would be spending more time on the estate, perhaps it was time to take another look.

"Your mother loved the ocean," my father murmured as we flew along the coastline from Santa Cruz to just south of San Simeon. His wistfulness renewed the regret I felt over not seeing her since the night of the Wicked Winemakers' Ball.

"Dad, why did you send your regrets rather than attend Ridge and Seraphina's wedding?"

When I glanced over to see if he'd heard me, I saw a tear run down his cheek.

"She wasn't feeling up to it. How I now wish I'd insisted she see a doctor."

"Hindsight is blind," I said, repeating one of her favorite expressions. My mother didn't believe in looking at the past with regret.

He nodded. "That's exactly what she would've said."

After landing the plane, I pulled it into the small hangar where I kept it stored and took our bags into the house.

"Shall we head straight to Butler Ranch?" my father asked.

I was elated he had before I got the chance, given only a half hour's drive separated Luisa and me.

"Sorcha said to come straight to the main residence when we arrive," I said, reading the message Jaicon sent shortly before we pulled through the ranch's gates.

"I can feel your happiness, Press. It fills my heart with joy."

It was, of course, tinged with regret, but it was unnecessary for me to say that to my father.

"You're going to love Luisa and her family, Dad."

"I've no doubt, son."

22

Luisa

"Ugh," I groaned inwardly, checking the clock fifteen minutes after I had the last time. It felt like the minutes were dragging when all I wanted to do was thank Sorcha and Bradley for once again hosting a crowd of people for dinner, then race over to the cottage where I was staying to wait for Press' call.

"What's wrong?" Seraphina asked.

"I'm tired. It feels more like ten o'clock than seven."

"I hear you. If I sat down right now, I'd probably fall asleep. It gets dark so early this time of year." She looked around the room. "Where's Jada?"

"She left earlier. She said to call if I needed her to come back, but I told her I'd be fine."

"Will you?"

"So far, so good."

She put her arm around my shoulders and squeezed. "I'm proud of you, sis."

I didn't want to admit the only reason I wasn't close to crawling out of my own skin was because Press and I had agreed to talk again tonight.

"I would love to know the story there," Seraphina said, motioning to the other side of the room, where Tryst and Jaicon stood, chatting.

"That reminds me. What do you know about Zin and Jada?"

Her eyes scrunched. "Nothing. Why?"

I told her about the odd exchange I'd witnessed between them earlier.

Before she could respond, we heard a knock at the front door. When Sorcha raced over and pulled it open, I gasped as my eyes met Press'.

"Hello, pet," he said when I rushed over, stopping right before I embarrassed myself by hugging him with all my might. "Luisa, I'd like you to meet my father, Martin. Dad, this is Luisa."

"It's a pleasure to finally meet you," said the man who I imagined Press would look identical to once he reached his father's age. They had the same deep-blue eyes, neatly trimmed facial hair, and similar height and builds. While lean, like a runner, I'd seen Press shirtless, and he had no shortage of muscle. Maybe he wasn't quite as buff as Beau, but his strength was evident.

"What are you doing here?" I asked after we awkwardly cheek-kissed.

"My father and I decided we could do with a visit to Seahorse."

I put one hand on my hip. "Funny you didn't mention it when we spoke earlier."

Press leaned in close so only I could hear him. "I thought it might be a nice surprise."

If I turned my face just slightly, I could kiss him. While it would probably shock the hell out of him to the point he might turn around and leave, the idea seemed perfectly natural to me. Maybe it was due to my mother and sister suggesting Press felt more for me than friendship. Or maybe it was because I hadn't been certain when I'd see him again, but God, did I want to throw my arms around him and tell him how happy I was he was here.

"I'd love to be able to read your mind, pet."

I smiled, looked him in the eye, and tucked my arm in his. "I'm glad you're here, Press."

"A good surprise, then?"

"The best."

Two hours ago, I couldn't wait for it to be late enough for me to return to the cottage. Now, I never wanted the night to end.

All around me, people were talking and laughing, drinking wine, and eating the food Sorcha and Bradley seemed to bring more of every five minutes.

All I could focus on, though, was the man sitting beside me. We'd remained close since he arrived, enough so that, sometimes, our arms or legs rested against each other's. I watched him as he spoke, how animated he was, the set of his lips when he smiled, even the crow's feet at the corner of his eyes I hadn't noticed until now.

Every so often, I breathed in the scent of him. As familiar as it was, the effect it had on me tonight was new. It made me want to wrap my arms around him and nuzzle my face into his neck.

From time to time, he'd glance at me, the expression on his face questioning. When he did, I'd start a conversation, drawing his attention to someone else in the room.

At ten o'clock, when the first guests left, Press looked over to his father, who sat talking to Laird, Tryst, Ridge's father, and Zin's father.

"I didn't realize they were friends," I commented.

"Very good friends, in fact. It's how Brix, Ridge, Zin, and I became close. Our families spent a great deal of time together."

When I leaned over and rested my head on his shoulder, Press kissed my forehead. It was something we'd done often, but tonight, it felt different. More intimate. Not at all fatherly or even big brotherly. I lifted my face to his in an open invitation to kiss me if he wanted to. He did, but instead of on my lips, he gave me a second smooch on my forehead.

"You're getting tired, pet. We should return to Seahorse."

It hadn't occurred to me he'd take me with him. "We?" I asked.

"Err…my dad and me. Unless you'd like to go too."

"I wouldn't want to intrude."

He cocked his head and smiled. "A recent, yet common, sentiment."

"Well, I don't."

"You're always welcome at Seahorse. I've told you so time and again."

I looked over at my mom and realized, if I left, she'd be here alone since Ridge and Seraphina said they were spending the night at their new house on See Canyon Road. "My mom," I said, sighing.

"Ah, I see. You don't think she'd fancy returning to the beach?"

"It's already so late. We'd need to pack a bag. It's probably too much of a hassle."

"Would you like me to convince you otherwise?"

"As much as I'd like to say yes, I'm not going to. I'll see you tomorrow, right?"

He nodded. "I received a message from Ares, saying your conversation is scheduled for zero eight hundred."

"Sorcha wants to be a part of it." I waited for Press to react, but he didn't. "Not surprised?" I asked.

"If Doc would allow it, I'm certain Sorcha would usurp Merrigan's role as managing partner of K19 Security Solutions."

"What do you say, son? Time to call it a night?" said Martin, approaching us.

"We should do." Press stood, holding his hand out to me. I stood too, and like earlier, he leaned in close. "Sure I can't convince you to come with us?"

The only thing I was sure of was if I did, I'd be tempted to crawl in bed with Press, invited or not. And it would be "not." He'd never once hit on me. Rather, he'd settled into the role of big brother, protector, and best friend. Until tonight, it was the only way I'd seen him. I couldn't expect him to have an instant epiphany like I had. And maybe tomorrow, when I saw him again, I wouldn't feel the same magnetic pull I felt now.

"Luisa?"

"Sorry. No, I can't."

"Understood." He looked across the room at Sorcha. "Shall I plan to return in time for your phone call, or would you prefer to handle it with Rua?"

"Rua?"

"I've heard a rumor it was her code name back in the day."

"Maybe I should ask her if she'd mind."

Press chuckled. "It's your phone call, pet."

"Right. Yes, I'd like you to be here, at least for moral support."

"Happy to be. Shall I walk you to the cottage before we leave?"

"Yes, please. I'll say good night first."

"As will I."

I tucked my arm in his like I had earlier and motioned to my mother, who nodded.

"It warms my heart to see you two together. We've missed you around here," Sorcha said to Press when he and I approached her.

I waited for him to argue, tell Sorcha we weren't "together," but he only thanked her for her hospitality.

"Are you stayin' here tonight, then?" she asked.

"At Seahorse. But I'll return before zero eight hundred."

"Shame," she said, nudging me with her elbow.

"Sorcha," Laird admonished.

She rolled her eyes and winked at me before saying good night.

"I fear Sorcha is getting the wrong idea about you and me," Press said when we followed my mother to the cottage's front door.

"She's not the only one," I mumbled more than said.

"My apologies."

"What for?"

"If people getting the wrong impression about you and me makes you uncomfortable."

"It doesn't." I leaned up, kissed his cheek, and went inside, closing the door behind me. Instinctively, I knew I didn't want to hear whatever he was about to say. I wanted to fall asleep thinking about how I felt when I was with him tonight. How it felt as though things had changed between us. And tomorrow, if we were back to however it was before, I'd accept it.

I'd just finished brushing my teeth, washing my face, and changing into the sweats and T-shirt I slept in when my phone vibrated. I threw myself on the bed and grabbed it, hoping it was Press, asking if I wanted him to read to me before I went to sleep.

Instead, when I swiped the screen, I screamed.

23

Press

The garage door had just closed behind us when my mobile rang. "It's Jaicon," I said to my father before answering.

"Press? Where are you?"

"We've just arrived at Seahorse."

"Is there a chance you can return to the ranch?"

My stomach dropped. "What's happened?"

"Luisa received a message from an unknown number on her cell phone. The team is trying to trace it now."

"I'm on my way." I didn't need to know what the message was. That she'd received one at all on a mobile she was given only a few days prior was alarming. No—it was terrifying.

"I'll go with you," my dad offered.

I reopened the garage door and backed into my driveway.

"Lavery? Perhaps I should drive."

I hadn't realized I was shaking to the point of it being visible, but I was. "Please. But you'll need to hurry."

"Understood."

We got out and switched seats. When my dad peeled onto the highway, I closed my eyes and held on tight. "It would be a good idea to keep it under one hundred and sixty kilometers," I suggested through gritted teeth.

"I thought you told me to hurry."

"Yes, Dad, but Luisa will need me to arrive in one piece."

He took his foot off the gas and slowed a little. However, if there were highway patrolmen on the road tonight, we'd be facing a speeding ticket for certain.

The gates opened as soon as we approached, and when we pulled up in front of the main residence, Jaicon and Tryst were waiting.

"Where is she?" I asked, jumping out of the car before my father came to a complete stop.

"Inside, with Sorcha and her mother." Tryst pointed, and I raced up the steps and through the door, not stopping to knock.

"Luisa?"

"Here," said Sorcha, motioning from the sofa where she and Luisa's mother crowded around her. Both women moved away when I sat down and took her in my arms. She wrapped hers around me and rested her head against my pounding heart.

"How did he get the number?" she cried.

"I don't know, but there's a team working to find out." While no one had said that specifically, I knew enough about Laird Butler to expect he wouldn't rest until he determined where the message had originated from.

"What if he knows where I am? Sends someone to get me?"

"We will not let that happen. You are safe, Luisa."

She raised her head; tears streaked her cheeks. "I can't stay here." She turned to Sorcha. "I'm sorry, but I can't."

"Aye, lass," Sorcha said, stroking her hair. "And you shan't. Naughton is on standby to take you wherever Press suggests."

Naughton Butler, who lived in the house we were in with his wife, Bradley, kept a helicopter here at the ranch. I'd seen it earlier this evening, when we arrived, and again just now.

"Thank you," I mouthed.

"We'll leave the two of you to talk," she said, leading Luisa's mother to the other side of the room.

"It was horrible," she cried.

I stroked her hair as Sorcha had, soothing her. "We do not have to talk about it now. Not unless you want to."

She shook her head vehemently. "I can't. Not ever."

"Then, you never shall."

I rocked her in my arms while she cried.

"I don't know what to do, where to go."

"We have options."

"Where?"

"Seahorse."

She shook her head. "It's too close."

"We could return to Napa."

"Are those the only two options?"

"While we won't be able to get there via helicopter,"—I smiled down at her—"we could also return to London."

"I have another suggestion," said Tryst, approaching us along with Jaicon.

My eyes bored into his. "Are you certain you can achieve the highest level of security?"

Tryst looked at Laird, who nodded. "I can assure you it is the *highest,* Press," Laird said. He rubbed his chin, something I'd seen him do often, and motioned to the door.

"Will you be okay if I step out for a moment?"

Luisa nodded. "For a moment."

Sorcha and Leah rushed over and sat on either side of her when I stood.

Laird, Tryst, Jaicon, and I went out to the porch. Tank and Zeppelin were there, waiting for us.

"The message originated from the Middle East," said Zeppelin. "Specifically, Egypt. The device used to contact Luisa was immediately destroyed. However, we're reaching out for help from our friends at the NRO."

My mind raced with what I knew about the lettered agency. Far more than I should, as a civilian, albeit one with intelligence connections.

Regardless of whether a device that had been used to transmit a message like the one Luisa received was destroyed, it would've still pinged cellular towers. It would be possible for an organization such as the National Reconnaissance Office to use triangulation and overheads—or satellites—to pass coordinates to theater assets—or drones—which could then be used to target the sender. None of this was public information, and it would be impossible to know if the man had what was referred to as "dirty knowledge," the very thing my mind raced with. If so, he would know what steps to take to go undetected.

I realized Zeppelin was speaking and I'd missed the bulk of it. "Sorry, can you please repeat?"

"Egypt is a tier-two country as far as human trafficking is concerned, but they're close to tier-three status."

"Is tier three the worst in terms of governmental intervention?" I asked.

"Correct. Wealthy gulf countries like Saudi Arabia and Kuwait are ranked tier three for abuse," said Zeppelin. "It's believed they get their victims in either Egypt or Iran, as does the UAE."

I wanted to clarify something. "Tier three for sexual abuse?"

"More than that, but in this case, I believe that's what we're dealing with. Females are sold into men's homes, then used up and essentially thrown away. Which subsequently feeds directly into street-level prostitution."

Based on Zeppelin's knowledge of human trafficking statistics, I began wondering who exactly the people on Luisa's detail were. Something told me they were far more than contractors for K19.

"I apologize for curtailing the conversation, but we've gone off track. The matter at hand is Luisa's relocation," said Jaicon.

"My apologies," I said to her before turning to Tryst. "I assume your suggestion is to return to Alamos."

Tryst nodded. "The decision is yours, of course."

I shook my head. "I mean no disrespect, but the decision is Luisa's."

"It's almost midnight," said Jaicon. "We should make a decision regarding relocation soon, even if it's temporary."

"Understood," I repeated. When I crossed the threshold and realized no one had followed, I closed the door behind me.

Sorcha stood when I approached, but Leah remained on the other side of her daughter.

"I'm sorry I didn't tell you, Mom. We didn't want you to worry," I heard her say when I sat beside her.

"It's okay, baby. You don't need to apologize."

Luisa's eyes met mine. "Mom, will you excuse us for a minute?"

Like before, Sorcha led Leah several feet away.

"If you'd like me to make the decision, I will. However, I'd like to hear your thoughts."

"I can't stay here tonight," she whispered. "I don't know if I'll sleep anyway, but I can't go back to that room."

"Would you feel safe if we stayed at Seahorse, just for the night, and made our decision in the morning?"

"Don't you have to return to Napa?"

"We can talk about that tomorrow as well, but the short answer is no, I do not."

"Would I be safe at your parents' place?"

"Yes." I didn't hesitate, given I could attest to the level of security in place. No one could get on or off the property undetected.

"That's where I'd like to go. *Tonight.*"

"We'll leave whenever you're ready. There's a helicopter waiting." I looked up when Jaicon came inside.

"We'll go to Napa," I told her.

"I need to pack," said Luisa.

"It's already taken care of," Jaicon assured her.

She looked over her shoulder. "Mom?"

"Don't worry about me, baby," said Leah. "I'll stay with Sorcha and Laird tonight, and in the morning, Ridge and Seraphina will come get me."

I leaned closer to Luisa. "The hour is late. If we're going to make the trip tonight, we should leave now."

She nodded and gripped my hand when we stood.

There was enough room in the helicopter to transport her, Jaicon, myself, and one other person.

"I'll ride with them," my father said, pointing to Tank and Magnet. Blackjack and Atticus were waiting in the second SUV, parked behind the first.

"I'll go with you if you're sure there's room," Zeppelin said to Naughton.

"You're up front with me," he responded.

The flight from Paso Robles to Napa seemed impossibly long in the helicopter. However, being able to land right on my parents' property saved an hour's drive from the airfield.

Luisa was quiet during the flight, but periodically, I reached over to squeeze her hand in reassurance.

I couldn't imagine how she must be feeling, particularly since I still didn't know exactly what the message she'd received said. Once we arrived and she was safely tucked away and asleep, I'd ask Jaicon for details.

Exhaustion was setting in on me as well. I'd slept restlessly, if at all, the last few days. While I didn't want to admit it, part of that was due to Luisa's absence.

When the helicopter landed on the front lawn, it dawned on me I hadn't given any thought to the sleeping arrangements. Not even as much as determining whether Luisa would stay in the guesthouse where she'd been before or in the main house. And while she'd managed in the guesthouse previously, with Jaicon and the rest of the team there with her, circumstances had changed quite drastically.

The other thing I was uncertain of was when my father would arrive with Tank, Magnet, Atticus, and

Blackjack. Regardless, I knew his main concern would be for Luisa's safety and well-being.

"Naughton? Would you like to stay the night and head back in the morning?" I asked.

"Appreciate it, but I told Bradley I'd be home in a few hours."

"I truly don't know how to thank you," I said, shaking his hand.

"It's what we do, right?"

I nodded. To my knowledge, no one in the Butler family had been a member of Los Caballeros. However, we'd certainly enlisted the aid of their family—Laird and Kade in particular—on several occasions.

I glanced over my shoulder and saw Jaicon was a few feet behind us, talking on her cell.

"We'll stay at the main residence tonight," I said to Zeppelin instead.

"Copy that, sir," he responded.

"Are you sure it's all right?" Luisa asked.

"Of course. There's plenty of room, and even if there weren't, all that matters is your safety."

I rested my palm on the pad near the front door, and it sprung open. I led Luisa inside. Jaicon and Zeppelin followed.

"I spoke with your father, who suggested you stay here this evening. Given they'll arrive close to dawn, he said he'd stay at Beau's," Jaicon reported.

It wasn't necessary for him to do so, but since the conversation had already taken place, I didn't see the need to contact him myself to argue about it.

I picked up Luisa's bag and led her upstairs. "Can I get you anything?" I asked.

"Where will I be staying?"

"There is a room adjacent to the one I'm in. It was Beau's when we were children. Thankfully, they've been redecorated to serve as guest rooms."

I opened the door, turned on the lights, and was happy to see the bed had been made, something that was definitely Mrs. Gonzales' doing, not my brother's. It also meant she'd changed the linens.

I pointed to an interior door. "That leads to the lavatory. I'm in the room just on the other side, but no worries about privacy. There's an additional door on my side with a lock."

She sighed. "I'm not worried about privacy, Press."

I set her bag on the chest at the end of the bed. "You must be exhausted. I'll let you get some rest. If you need anything at all, I'm just through there."

She stood where she was, hugging herself and biting her lower lip.

"Luisa?"

Her eyes filled with tears.

"Come here." I pulled her into my arms. "Tell me what you need, pet."

"I'm scared," she said, barely above a whisper.

"You don't have to be alone. I can ask Jaicon to—"

She shook her head.

"What if we read a bit?" I offered.

"You wouldn't mind?"

"I'm still tightly wound from the trip myself. It will help us both rest more easily. I'll get my tablet from the other room. It'll take but a minute," I added when I pulled away, but her hand gripped mine. "Well, then, how about if you come with me?"

"Hang on."

I waited while Luisa kicked off her shoes and removed her jacket, then I led her through the doors connecting the two rooms. Once we'd entered mine, she dropped my hand.

"This room feels different."

I walked over to the table where my tablet sat, took off my own shoes, and dropped my jacket on the chest at the end of my bed. "How so?"

"Warmer."

"If you'd prefer it, we can read in here. You can stay in here as well."

"Will you stay, Press?"

My back was to her when she asked, and I was thankful for it. I closed my eyes, breathed in deeply, and reminded myself that to Luisa, I was her safety net, her protector, and while she may consider me a father figure, if I had to choose, I'd prefer older brother. Not that I wanted to be either.

The desire I felt for her was completely inappropriate. She needed comfort and reassurance.

The first time we lay in each other's arms, I was overcome by grief and exhaustion after learning my mother had passed. She'd comforted me that night. Could I do the same for her now? Could I set aside the longing I felt, or would my body react of its own accord to the woman I hungered for? A kiss alone or a touch—skin to skin—would likely bring me to the epitome of pleasure.

It had been four months since I stopped seeing the last woman who'd been my lover. I hadn't thought of her once since I first met Luisa the night she walked out of the shipping container, broken. Then, I only wanted to protect her, help her heal, be someone she felt safe with.

As she recovered, she became a woman I desired more than any other I'd ever known. It went beyond that, though. I'd fallen in love with her.

24

Luisa

I waited for Press to turn around, wishing he'd do it before he had the chance to mask whatever it was he was really feeling. There were times I'd noticed his expression go entirely blank. Not that I'd point it out.

Now, I longed for some sign of what my mother and sister insisted I was too blind to see.

When he'd bounded in the door after having left Butler Ranch less than an hour before, all I could think of was that I wanted him to hold me in his arms and never let go.

If I'd told him so, it wouldn't have surprised him. He'd done it countless times before. It had changed for me, though. Yes, I wanted and needed his comfort, but earlier, what I felt more was desire. It made no sense, but the only way I could block what I'd seen in the message earlier was to focus entirely on Press. As long as he was within reach, the panic remained at bay. What I felt for him eclipsed everything else.

"Press?"

"I heard you, pet."

My eyes met his when he turned around. Our gazes remained riveted as he walked toward me.

"Are you warm enough?" he asked, stopping close enough to touch, to kiss.

"I'm fine," I lied. I was shivering, but not because of the room's temperature. It was Press' nearness.

"I could light a fire," he offered.

"That would be nice," I murmured, leaning forward just slightly, wishing he'd do the same, that our lips would brush one another's. Somehow, I knew it would be entirely different than Beau's kiss.

"Would you like to use the lavatory or perhaps change into something more comfortable?"

I shook my head. "I changed and brushed my teeth earlier. You know…before."

"Understood," he said, setting the tablet on the table he'd picked it up from before pulling a chair closer to the bed.

"You don't want to lie down?"

"Go ahead, pet. I'll get the fire going."

I walked around the chair, folded back the sheets, and nestled under them. I watched him kneel down, pull the screen open, and light the kindling. How hadn't I noticed his broad shoulders before? Or his lean hips and long legs, covered by jeans that fit as if they'd been custom-tailored? When he stood and turned toward me, my breath quickened as I stared into eyes flaming with the desire my sister insisted he felt. Shamelessly, I wanted to suck on the tongue that peeked out to moisten his lower lip.

I realized then that no man had ever affected me the way Press did. I'd never yearned for one's touch the way I did his. At a time when my body should be frozen in terror, I was burning inside.

I blinked, and when my eyes met his again, he'd masked whatever was there only moments ago. Or had I imagined it?

Disappointment settled in place of my want as he sat in the chair after picking up his tablet.

He cleared his throat and began reading. I rested my head on the pillow and closed my eyes, knowing if I didn't, they'd fill with tears. Soon, the lilt of his voice gave me the comfort I needed to drift to sleep.

When I woke, the room was flooded with daylight and the chair sat empty. I could hear someone I assumed was Press moving about in the room he'd first taken me to last night. The doors were open between the two, and as he walked past, our eyes met.

"What time is it?" I asked, sitting up when he entered the room.

"Almost ten."

"I'm sorry I slept so long."

Press shook his head. "Don't be. I'm glad you were able to rest."

I glanced at the other side of the bed. The pillows were perfectly fluffed, and there was no sign anyone had lain there.

"I, uh, eventually slept in Beau's room," he said when my eyes returned to his.

"Did your father get home okay?" I asked, not knowing what else to say.

"Yes. They pulled in around five this morning."

"Wait, did you say it's ten?" I gasped. "I missed my call with the profilers!"

"I contacted Ares. They are in the midst of investigating last evening's occurrences and have suggested postponing indefinitely."

I shuddered when I recalled the message I'd received and put my hand on my stomach when I felt like I might be sick.

"My apologies for bringing it up," Press said, walking over to the chair he'd been sitting in when I went to sleep. "However, if you want to talk about it, now or later, we can. It also occurred to me you may want to schedule a call with Dr. Benedict."

"What day is it?" I asked, still groggy.

"Saturday. New Year's Eve."

"She won't be in the office until Monday."

"I've been in contact with her, and she assured me she'd be available to speak with you today, tomorrow, or anytime you'd like."

It would probably be a good idea if I did. Not because I *wanted* to talk about the message. I *needed* to talk to her about Press. "I'd like to."

"I can take care of scheduling it. Or you can, obviously."

I smiled. Press was always the protector, always hiding behind the mask of propriety. I longed to see him drop his shield, let loose, and show me the man behind the steely facade. Would he, though? Could he ever allow himself to be unguarded? Vulnerable?

Something told me I'd have to be the one to strip away his defenses. He'd never put me in a position of having to reject him, especially given I'd been forthcoming about the crush I used to have on Beau.

"Would you like some coffee? Breakfast, perhaps?"

I hadn't thought I'd be able to eat anything, but at the mention of food, my stomach rumbled. "I guess so," I said.

"I'll bring it up to you, and don't worry about being alone. Jaicon is in the hall beyond the doorway."

"I'll come down with you. Actually, I'll meet you in the kitchen after I've used the *lavatory*."

He smiled when I mimicked his accent. "See you shortly, then." He walked through the bathroom and closed the farthest door behind him.

After taking a quick shower, brushing my teeth, and putting on a change of clothes, Jaicon and I went downstairs. Press wasn't alone in the kitchen. He and Zeppelin were head-to-head in the midst of a serious-looking conversation. I thought about turning around to give them privacy, but Press noticed us before I could.

"Did something else happen?" I asked when neither dropped their somber expression.

"Not at all. Zeppelin has brought you a new phone. And just for your peace of mind, it's been set to block any unknown numbers."

I thought about Beau when he handed it to me, and I thanked him. I had no reason to believe he'd call again, but if he wanted to, he wouldn't have the new number. It occurred to me then that I didn't tell Press I'd spoken to him. "Have you programmed in the same numbers as before?" I asked.

"I have done," Zeppelin responded. "If there's nothing else, I'll check in later."

Press poured a cup of coffee and added a teaspoon of sugar and a splash of cream before handing it to me.

"My apologies. Breakfast was waylaid by my conversation." I knew Press well enough to see there was something more he wasn't telling me. It had been at least twenty minutes since he came downstairs.

"It took all that time to talk about a replacement phone?" I said, my eyes boring into his.

"He had an update to share regarding my brother as well."

"Which reminds me. He called yesterday afternoon."

Press had been taking things out of the refrigerator, but stopped and closed the door. "What did he say? Do you mind my asking?"

"He apologized. Mainly for the kiss, but also for treating me unfairly. His words, by the way, not mine."

"I see," Press muttered, reopening the refrigerator. He stood in front of it but didn't appear to be removing anything else.

"Press?"

He looked over his shoulder at me.

"I feel like there's something you're not telling me."

He shook his head, but his lack of response made me uncomfortable.

"I changed my mind. I'm not hungry." I picked up my coffee and left the room. When I reached the stairs, I decided I didn't want to return to his bedroom. Instead, I went to the room he'd taken me to the night his mother died.

While he'd mentioned there was a view of the vineyards, I hadn't expected it to take my breath away the way it did. The windows lining the outer wall were in a semicircle, which I hadn't realized when they were covered by blinds.

I walked over, sipped my coffee, and took in the scenery. I understood why this had been Mrs. Barrett's favorite room. And how thoughtful it had been of Press' father to have it enclosed for her. It was the kind of thing Press would do.

"My mum would've adored you," I heard him say from behind me. "I regret the two of you never met."

My eyes filled with unexpected tears, spilling over onto my cheeks.

"Please don't cry," he said, coming to stand beside me.

"I'm the reason you hadn't seen her since the night of the auction."

"Luisa—"

"It's true, Press. Don't deny it."

"She understood. She also knew I was on my way here. I can only hope that filled her with some comfort."

I turned and put my arms around him. "I wish I could've met her too."

Like always, Press returned the embrace. "You remind me of her. I told her that."

I raised my head from his chest and looked up at him. "How do I remind you of her?" I asked. Rather than fishing for compliments, I was curious.

He tightened his arms. "I told her you were amazing. Brave, strong, funny, and…gorgeous."

I pulled back a second time and stared into his eyes. "You think I'm gorgeous?"

He smiled. "Come, now, Luisa. There isn't a man alive who wouldn't agree with me."

"Was there anything else you told her?"

He studied me, his eyes darting back and forth between mine. I could see the war waging behind them.

"Tell me, Press," I whispered.

His brow furrowed.

I leaned up and brushed his lips with mine, then his cheek. "Tell me," I repeated, this time whispering in his ear.

I could feel the change in his body. It was rock-hard from tension, then it was as if he'd suddenly let it go.

"I told her Beau doesn't care for you the way I do."

I held him tighter and rested my head above his heart.

"Luisa…I need you to look at me." He waited until I did. "You kissed me."

I nodded. "I kissed you." I lowered my arms so they were around his waist.

"Why?"

"Because I care for you too, Press."

He didn't speak, nor did he do the one thing I really wanted him to do. I moved one hand to his neck and pulled him close enough that I could kiss his other cheek.

"How do you care about me? Like a sister?"

He shook his head.

"How, Press?"

"Like this." He lowered his lips to mine and licked my lips with his tongue as though he was demanding entrance. When I opened to him, it moved against mine, tentative at first, then more demanding.

Press was kissing me, and it felt so right. Better than right. It was perfect. I wove my fingers in his hair, determined to hold him there if he tried to pull away. He didn't. He kept kissing me. It was slow, languorous, breathtaking. And then it wasn't. His mouth plundered mine, and I returned the kiss with all the passion he'd unleashed.

We both startled and took a step back when we heard the front door open and footsteps headed in our direction.

"Lavery, Luisa, forgive the interruption," Martin said, looking from his son to me, then back again.

"Not at all, Father. Good morning."

"Good morning," he responded.

I turned toward the window, knowing my cheeks were flushed and my lips swollen from Press' ravishing.

"I was about to make breakfast if you'd like to join us," Press offered.

"Much appreciated, but I think I'll retire to my room and get some more rest."

"Of course. Sleep well."

I didn't say anything or turn around even after the sound of his footfalls grew fainter.

"Luisa, I—"

I looked over my shoulder at him. "Press, if you apologize, I swear I'll throttle you."

He turned me in his arms. "I will never regret kissing you."

"You make it sound as though it won't happen again."

25

"Nothing could be further from what I desire."

"Then, kiss me again."

As I lowered my mouth to hers, something outside caught my eye. What in the bloody hell was my brother doing back, and why *now,* of all times?

I brushed her lips, then pulled away.

"What's wrong?"

"Beau," I said, motioning with my head.

"He's here?" she gasped.

My gut clenched, wondering if Luisa would be the one regretting our kiss. "It appears so."

"I thought…It doesn't matter what I thought."

The front door opened, but she didn't release her hold from around my waist even when I relaxed my arms.

"Anyone home?" Beau hollered from the foyer.

"In here," I shouted back, turning both Luisa and me to face the room's entrance. My arm remained around her shoulders and hers around my waist.

"Hi," he said, stopping before coming all the way into the room. "I'd ask if I'm interrupting, but…" Rather than finish his sentence, he laughed. When neither Luisa nor I made any move to separate, Beau cocked his head.

"I'm pleased you've returned," I said, only then releasing her to walk over to embrace him. "Father will be as well."

"I got as far as London," he said, looking over at Luisa, who'd turned her back to us. "Then I realized there were things here I needed to rectify."

"Should I ask what specifically?"

Beau sighed. "I know this may sound odd, but I feel as though I am interrupting. Is there something going on between the two of you?"

"You're not interrupting," said Luisa, turning to face him after clearing her throat. There was a smile on her face, but there was no warmth behind it. "What things do you need to rectify?" she asked.

He took several steps in her direction. "Mainly, things between you and me."

Luisa's eyes met mine, then she glanced at Beau. I nodded, guessing she wished to speak with him alone.

"If you'll excuse me, I'll let the two of you talk." I hurried out of the room, knowing I wouldn't be able to bear it if Beau's return meant the short-lived romance between us came to a quick and bitter end.

I raced up the stairs to his room and removed my clothes from it. The question then was what to do with Luisa's bag. She'd moved it into my room after I came downstairs to start breakfast—something I still hadn't done.

I went across the hall, to a spare bedroom, opened the door, and tossed my bag and clothes on the bed, then went back for my tablet and laptop.

Perhaps the lack of sleep was affecting me more than I'd realized. I had no idea what to do.

Last night, after Luisa had nodded off, I read a few minutes longer, just in case she woke up. At the same time, I sent a text to Jaicon, asking what the message Luisa had received from the unknown number said.

That was what Zeppelin and I had been discussing before Luisa and Jaicon came into the kitchen earlier.

"A graphic and disturbing photo accompanied the message," he'd told me.

"May I see it?" I'd asked.

"I'll forward it to you."

I hadn't had the chance to look before, so I picked up my mobile and swiped the screen. There was an alert that I'd received a message, and I saw it was from him.

Again, the image is graphic and disturbing. I warn you not to view it in Luisa's presence, it read.

I downloaded and opened it. It was grainy and difficult to decipher. However, in it was a naked woman, who thankfully, had a different height and build than Luisa. Her arms and legs were bound and spread, tied to four hooks protruding from the wall she faced. There were marks crisscrossing her back that appeared to be bleeding. The only other thing visible in the photo was a man's hand holding some kind of whip.

The accompanying message read, "Your punishment awaits, my Luisa. Next time, you won't escape before we've had our fun."

I rushed into the lavatory, closed the door behind me, and wretched. Even after I'd emptied the meager contents of my stomach, I continued to heave.

When I exited the washroom after rinsing my mouth, Luisa was standing in the hallway just outside the bedroom door. Her eyes were wide.

"You saw it," she said.

Without answering, I took her hand and pulled her into my arms. "I will protect you. I will keep you safe. I vow it on my own life."

"Don't say that," she whispered. "I can't lose you, Press."

"You never will. I'll be at your side, watching over you for as long as you'll allow me to be. Even if…" I regretted my final two words as soon as I'd spoken them.

She raised her head from the familiar place it rested above my heart. "Even if? What were you about to say? Even if I'm with Beau?"

I nodded slowly. "No matter who you may choose, I'll still be here for you."

"Choose? Am I choosing?"

"A poor choice of words, I'm afraid. Not at all what I meant."

"Is that who you think I am, Press? Do you think I could kiss you like I did, then rush into Beau's arms the minute I saw him?"

"No. I don't. I—"

"I told you I didn't want him to kiss me. Did you think I was lying?" Luisa grabbed my arms and removed them from around her body, then she brushed past me, raced out the door, and hurried down the staircase.

I'd grown so used to letting her go, giving her space, that it was what I almost did.

"Don't let her go," I heard my mother's voice say in my head.

I rushed after her, following when she ducked into the room where we'd shared our first kiss, also the room where we'd first slept side by side. It was already my favorite in the entire house, but now was more so.

"There's something I need to tell you," I said, walking over to where she looked out the window, crying.

She turned to face me. "What?"

"I wasn't entirely honest with you earlier when I told you what I'd said to my mum about you."

Her mouth gaped as if she was preparing to give me another tongue-lashing.

"Please let me finish. I told you I said Beau didn't care about you the way I did. What I really said was that Beau doesn't *love* you the way I do."

"Then, how could you think—"

"Because I'm a bloody idiot. Because I never thought you'd see me as a man you desired rather than an older brother."

She silently studied me while I held my breath, awaiting her response. "I believe you," she finally said.

"You do?"

Luisa nodded. "Do you want to know why?"

"Because you know I'd never lie to you?" I hung my head. "Except for the one time I just admitted I did."

"That isn't why. I believe you because you interrupted me. Well, first, you followed me. *Then* you interrupted me."

I put one arm around her. "That, somehow, means I'm worthy of you believing me?"

"You've never done either before. You wouldn't allow yourself to."

"In the past, I wanted to…"

"Give me space?"

"Yes," I admitted.

"Do you know how badly I wanted you to let your guard down? To chase after me? To interrupt me?"

Rather than respond, I let go of the reins I continued to hold and kissed her. "I dreamed of this," I confessed against her lips. "Every night."

"I didn't know. I didn't see it." She rested her palm on my cheek. "I stupidly thought I wanted Beau when, all this time, it's been you, Press. You who I talked to about everything. Every fear, every desire, every time I couldn't make up my mind, every time I doubted myself. Never once did you waver. You were there for me whenever I needed you and even when I didn't realize how much I did. How could I have been so blind?"

"You weren't blind, Luisa. You were healing. You're still healing."

"Thanks to you," she said, leaning up to kiss me.

"Not me alone."

She rested her hands on my chest. "At the wedding, when you said you were leaving but nothing about when we'd see each other again, I felt like a part of me was dying. And then, when I had to go to Butler Ranch to give you the time and space to mourn your mother, I realized I left a part of me behind."

"I felt the same way."

"When Sorcha opened the door and you walked in, last night, I'd never been so happy to see anyone in my life. I mean that, Press. Even when I saw Seraphina after the container door opened and I walked out. Nothing has hit me the way seeing you did. I wanted to race into your arms and beg you to never leave me again."

"I won't leave you. I promise." Something about the words I'd just spoken didn't ring true. I meant them. I'd never abandon Luisa willingly. But deep inside, the possibility I'd have to leave her unwillingly settled like a blanket of dread.

"I want to tell you about my conversation with Beau."

Thankfully, we'd already confessed our feelings for one another. If we hadn't, I would've dreaded whatever she was about to tell me.

"He came back for me. He was considering going to Australia, as everyone suspected he might, but instead, he came back here. He told me he'd like us to see each other, um, romantically."

If I didn't know it was me she wanted, her last words would have gutted me. "What was your response?"

"Obviously, I told him I wasn't interested. However, something he said resonated with me."

"Go on."

"He said he knew the day would come when I would be brave enough to admit my feelings for you."

Admittedly, that my brother would say such a thing stunned me.

"He was right, Press. It took a lot for me to just admit I missed you."

"It was the same for me, pet."

"I need to warn you, though; he's hurt and angry. Those words weren't spoken kindly. More, accusatory."

Luisa tightened her grip around my waist, perhaps guessing I intended to go in search of my brother and give him the punch in the face he deserved.

"He's talking to your father now, then I'm pretty sure he's leaving again."

"I should speak with him before he does."

"Please don't argue with him. Focus on the motivation behind the behavior, not the behavior itself."

I looked at her with wide eyes. "My mum used to say that very thing."

"I think most mothers do." She smiled. "He's hurting, Press, just like you are."

"He and our mother were quite close."

"You were close to her too."

I nodded. "She was our anchor, something Beau required more often than I did."

"That doesn't come as a surprise. You're my anchor."

I leaned down and kissed her. "I want to be so much more. If that's what you want as well."

"I do…" She bit her bottom lip.

"But we need to take things slowly," I finished her sentence.

"You understand me better than anyone, even Dr. Benedict."

"Would you still like to arrange a talk with her?" I asked.

"I would."

"Can I assist in any way?"

Luisa smiled. "I'm really proud of you right now, Press. You didn't automatically set about arranging an appointment for me."

"Would *you* like to do that now?" I asked.

"Yes, and after that, we need to get to work."

I cocked my head.

"Last night, you asked if I could start today, and I told you I could."

"I was being facetious, Luisa."

She pulled away and folded her arms. However, behind her smile, I saw all the warmth that had been missing when she smiled at my brother earlier.

"Go talk to Beau," she said, taking a step back. "I'll meet you back here, and you can show me your office."

As I walked away, I realized I'd have to find a place here, on the grounds, where Luisa and I could work together. I wasn't here often enough to have an office per se. I set up my laptop pretty much anywhere and did what needed to be done.

Beau had an office in the winery building. There were several reasons I wouldn't be interested in making use of it.

I reached the bottom of the staircase at the same time my brother did.

"Do you have a few minutes for us to talk?"

He looked at his mobile. "Not really. I need to leave now to catch my flight."

"Where are you headed?" I asked, wishing my brother would make eye contact with me rather than looking everywhere else. "Beau?"

"I don't know."

"Yet you have a flight to catch."

"Sod off, Lavery."

"Boys," I heard my father say from the top of the stairs. It was a tone of voice we'd heard often when we were growing up.

"Sorry, Father," I said, looking up at him.

"Sorry, Father," Beau mimicked under his breath.

"I'd like to take flowers to your mother's grave. Will the two of you join me?"

Thankfully, Beau didn't check his mobile or give the excuse he needed to leave to catch a flight.

My father put one arm around my shoulders and the other around my brother's. "Your mother had a tradition when one year ended and another began. Do you recall what it was?"

I almost laughed at the way he was speaking to us as though we were five-year-olds.

"Out with the old and in with the new," Beau answered.

"Precisely. If she were here, she'd tell you both to let go of the things that angered you in the past in order to make room for the joy to come in the new year."

"Not quite so easy this year, Dad," I said.

"When it isn't easy, it's the best time to do it."

26

Luisa

From my perch near the window, I watched Press, Beau, and their father walk across the lawn, heading away from the house. I wondered what Martin was saying to them. Whatever it was, I hoped it would help smooth things over between his two sons.

It was impossible not to hear the argument they'd had when Press left the room. It was short, but the animosity in Beau's voice was evident, and it angered me.

I'd spent weeks wishing he'd notice me, pay attention to me, want to be with me. While he flirted, enough to hold my attention, he'd never taken it further. In fact, when he showed up at Seahorse with his girlfriend, I felt like a fool for misreading what I thought were signs he was interested in me. I was so embarrassed, so humiliated, I wanted to leave immediately.

Thinking back on it, I cringed. I'd never considered how much my actions must've hurt Press. He'd done so much for me, and I'd shown so little appreciation.

The bottom line, in my opinion anyway, was Beau had no right to be angry. In fact, I wondered if he had an inkling Press and I were getting close and if that was the only reason he'd kissed me the way he had, in full view of his brother.

I'd sent a message to Dr. Benedict as soon as Press left the room. While he'd said she would be available to talk with me today or tomorrow, I wouldn't count on it. It was a Saturday during the holiday season.

Even if she did respond and had time to talk, we would have to do it over the phone since I still hadn't remembered to charge my tablet.

"Anything I can help with?" Jaicon asked.

I smiled. "Do I appear perplexed?"

She smiled too. "Very much so."

"I'm waiting to hear from my therapist," I confessed.

"It's important you reach out to people like that, those able to help you."

"I want to talk to her about Press more than I do about the message I received last night." In fact, I never wanted to think or talk about that ever again.

"He cares about you very much," Jaicon said, motioning to the three men almost out of view.

"I've finally realized how much he does."

"You're nice together." Her expression changed as if she suddenly remembered she was on the job. "Not that it's my business."

"I don't mind. I like having someone to talk to."

"We could arrange for Jada to join you here if it would help."

"I appreciate the offer, but she's already done so much for me. I don't want her to have to come all the way up here." My cell phone vibrated with a message from Dr. Benedict. "I should respond to this," I said to Jaicon.

"Please do so. I'm in the vicinity, should you need anything."

I thanked her, then read the message the therapist sent. She reiterated she was available to speak whenever I was ready. Rather than respond immediately, I hesitated. There were two subjects she'd want to talk about. First, the message. Second, Press.

I found myself dreading discussing either with her, even though only a few minutes ago, I'd wanted to talk about him. Wouldn't talking with her when I didn't want to, be counterproductive?

I sighed in relief when I saw Press headed this way. Beau trailed behind him, talking to Martin. None of the three looked particularly tense, which I hoped meant they'd set aside their differences. Their family needed to band together now. I remembered as much from my father's accident. We'd needed to come together, but we hadn't. Seraphina was the one who'd stepped in to fill the void left by my parents—one who was in a coma and the other who might as well have been since she sat by his side day in, day out. It hadn't gotten much better after he died.

I lived with my mom while I was in college, but we certainly didn't have a good relationship. Before I was abducted, we'd argued more than spoke. Since I'd been rescued, things were a lot better, but was that because she was babying me? Was everyone babying me?

"You're frowning."

I nearly fell off the window seat when I turned my head and saw Press standing within a foot of me. I hadn't heard the front door open nor him walking into the room.

"My apologies. I didn't intend to startle you. What's on your mind, Luisa?"

"I'd say that should be obvious, but you know better, don't you?" I took a deep breath and let it out slowly. "My mom."

"May I sit?" he asked.

"You don't have to ask to sit beside me, Press," I said, knowing he would continue to, regardless. He was polite and considerate and cared more about me than anyone else in my life ever had. Besides Seraphina. And Jada. But even she didn't know me as well as Press did.

He rested his hand on my cheek. "Don't bite your lip, pet." His eyes were soft and warm and so full of what I now knew was love for me. I was ashamed I hadn't noticed what everyone else had.

"I watched the three of you leave, earlier, then also when you returned. You seemed more relaxed than when you left."

"We visited my mum's grave. In the past, I believed it odd when I saw other people do it, but I found it quite therapeutic."

"I'm glad," I said.

"Tell me what this has to do with your mother."

"Your family needs to band together right now. I'd hate for you and Beau to be fighting because of me."

"Beau…"

I studied him as he collected his thoughts. Lavery Barrett was the best man—the best person—I knew. He didn't just spout off about whatever his brother had done to irritate him, at least not now, when we were talking about them banding together.

"I encouraged him to go. Without rancor, in case you're wondering. I didn't say this to him, but there's something missing in my brother's life, and while he may think he'll find it with another person—a woman in particular—my belief is everything he truly needs is inside of him." His eyes met mine, and rather than hurt or pain, I saw acceptance. "I sound like my mum."

"She was a smart woman."

"Indeed."

"What about you, Press? Is there anything missing in your life?" It was a risky question for me to ask. If he said there was, our relationship would end before it truly began.

"I learned a great deal about myself while spending time with you," he said.

"What not to do?" I attempted a joke, but it fell flat.

"You are so much more than you realize, Luisa Reeve. And, no, I've never once disagreed with a course of action you took. I may not have always liked it, but I respected your decisions."

"Thank you, Press."

"As I watched you overcome an ordeal unimaginable to most everyone, it inspired me to believe in myself more. What I'm capable of." He leaned forward and kissed my forehead. "I also learned patience wasn't my greatest strength."

"You're remarkably patient with me."

"Because I care too much about you to push when you're not ready."

"I'm avoiding Dr. Benedict," I confessed.

"Ah. I see. You're avoiding the things you'd rather not talk about with Dr. Benedict."

"Truth."

"Can I be a sounding board?" he asked.

"One of the subjects is you, Press."

"Tell me what you fear Dr. Benedict will say concerning me."

"That I rely too much on you."

Press nodded. "And what will she say about this shift in our relationship?"

"Probably something about hero worship or falling in love with my caregiver, or maybe that I have a daddy complex."

"Ouch," he said, rubbing his chest but still smiling.

"I'm telling you what I think Dr. Benedict will say, not how I feel."

"What would you say in response?"

"I woke up. Or my body did. Every part of me, actually. Maybe it was a good thing Beau kissed me."

Press shook his head. "I will never agree that was a good thing."

"Even if it made me realize I wasn't as attracted to him as I thought?"

He sighed. "I suppose. However, I would've preferred you come to that realization without me having to witness my brother doing what I'd dreamed so often of."

"You don't have to dream anymore. You can kiss me whenever you'd like. Say, for example, now."

He leaned forward, and our lips met. Too briefly for me, but Press was onto what I was up to. Distraction.

"So that was it?" he asked. "One kiss from Beau, and you suddenly changed your mind about him?"

"Being away from you is what changed my mind. Or made me think, anyway." I took his hands in mine. It was something he always did with me when he wanted me to pay close attention to what he was saying. "I missed you so much. I know I've already told you I did, but I doubt you know the extent of it. I ached. Here." I brought his hand to my heart. "Ached, Press."

"Luisa—"

I put my finger on his lips. "I have so much more I want to say."

He nodded.

"I never felt that way about Beau. When Daphne showed up at Seahorse and I saw them together, I was humiliated and embarrassed more than hurt. I recognize that now. I also recognize how much I must've hurt you."

"I understood."

"You understood about Beau, but after all you'd done for me, how you'd been there for me, I just left."

"The move to Butler Ranch proved a positive thing for you."

"I agree. However, there wasn't a day when I didn't speak with you. I don't remember many when you didn't drive over and spend the better part of the day with me."

"I couldn't bear to be away from you."

"It hit me when we were in Mexico. When you said you were leaving and had no plans to return, I was so angry with you for not telling me."

He smiled. "I recall. You may not appreciate hearing this, but I was proud of you. You had every right to call me out for not informing you. It was the antithesis of how our friendship had been to that point. I was glad you didn't just lie down and take it, so to speak."

"What made you want to leave, Press?"

He took my hand and brought it to his heart. "I looked up at you during the ceremony. At first I thought you were looking at me. Then I realized it was Beau you were enraptured with. My decision to leave was about self-preservation."

My eyes filled with tears. "I'm sorry."

"I cannot accept your apology. You had no idea how I felt about you."

"Why didn't I? Everyone else knew."

He brushed a tear from my cheek. "Perhaps you weren't ready."

"And you care about me too much to push when I'm not ready," I repeated the words he'd said a few minutes ago.

Press nodded.

"I agree, in part. However, it had to be more than just missing you. Even before Beau kissed me—sorry," I said when he cringed. "I'd already started thinking of you differently."

He sat back and shook his head.

"What?" I asked.

"Something Zin said."

"Will you tell me?"

"We were still in Mexico. He said Beau was safe."

"Beau? Safe?" I said with wide eyes.

"Close to my response."

"What was your response?"

"I told him he had it backwards. Perhaps not those exact words. However, I said it was I who was safe."

"Did he say anything else?"

Press nodded. "He told me I was looking at it wrong."

I leaned up and kissed him. "Press, there's one thing that's still bothering me."

"Out with it," he said, winking.

"What you said about choosing."

The smile left his face, and he looked into my eyes. "I regret those words very much, Luisa. I meant nothing against you—"

"That's the part that bothers me. You meant nothing against me, which means you didn't—couldn't—believe I'd want *you*."

"My father approached me the day after my mother passed. You'd just left for Butler Ranch." Press took several deep breaths. "This is harder than I expected it to be."

I tightened my grip on his hands and waited.

"It was after the kiss." He hung his head. "I still regret not seeing you off."

I blinked in an effort not to cry again. "You were hurting."

"As I said, my father approached me. He'd actually heard me arguing with Zin. He said, 'I'm going to give you the same advice your mother would. She'd tell you to step in front of your brother, not to the side.'"

Hearing the anguish in his voice wrecked me. "I'm so sorry."

"It's what I've always done, you see. I never fought for what I wanted. If Beau expressed an interest, I stepped aside."

"Press, I…I don't know what to say."

"How do you feel about me, Luisa?"

I brushed my tears away. "I'm not sure I have a grasp on how love feels, exactly. But I do know this. You're the person I want to see every day. Be with. Talk to. Share my life with." I bit my bottom lip, but I was determined to continue, no matter how hard the words were for me to say. "You're the person I want to make love with, Press. No one else."

27

Press

Desire surged through my body. "Luisa, I never imagined—well, maybe I imagined—but I never believed I'd hear you say any of what you just said. My God, I'm speechless."

"How do you feel about me, Press?"

She hadn't given me platitudes; her words had meaning, and she deserved the same from me. Thus, I needed to think before I spoke.

"There are three simple words that carry the weight of thousands, even millions. 'I love you' feels so inadequate, yet heaping on adjectives diminishes the magnitude of the emotion." My eyes bored into hers. "I love you, Luisa. Everything about you. Even the things you don't love about yourself. Or perhaps especially those things because each facet of your personality makes up the wonder of who you are."

Her cheeks turned a delightful shade of pink. "Thank you, Press."

"What you said about making love…"

"Did I make you uncomfortable?"

"Perhaps a bit. Please do not take this as a rejection of your desire. My body is one hundred percent in favor of lifting you in my arms, carrying you upstairs to my bed, and spending the entirety of the day learning every nuance of you. My heart and brain, though, aren't ready."

"I understand."

"That you do, does not surprise me in the least. You know me so well, and while the same can be said about me with you, I want to know even more. You're my closest friend, the person I feel safest sharing my feelings with. Since the moment we met, I felt as though I was put on this planet to protect you. Loving you has given my life meaning beyond what I knew existed. This change, our admission of feelings, is new, and I want to savor it."

"This may sound as though I'm only trying to save face, but when I said you're the only man I want to make love with, what I meant is forever, Press, not necessarily today."

Her eyes hadn't wavered from mine. Had she even blinked? I was astonished by how in tune we were with each other, and yet, we'd both misread the other's feelings for so long. It was the reason for my desire to spend time getting to know one another on a romantic level before jumping straight into the sack.

"Does this mean we're boyfriend and girlfriend?" Luisa asked.

"If you'll have me."

"I'll keep you as long as you'll let me."

Forever sounded damn good to me. "Is there anything special you'd like to do tonight?"

"I've never been big on celebrating New Year's Eve. What about you?"

"There are a handful of family traditions my mother insisted on when we were home. My father mentioned one to my brother and me on our walk."

"Will you tell me what it is?"

"Of course. We'd either think of or write down the things that angered, hurt, or frustrated us. Then, sometime before the last day of the year, we'd let it all go to make room for joy in the coming year."

"I like that tradition. Did you share the things you wrote down with each other?"

"Sometimes. Sometimes not. My mum gave us the choice."

By the way her eyes lit up, I knew it was something she wanted to do. While I'd told my father it might be difficult to make room for joy this year, as I thought about it, there were a good number of things I wanted to bid good riddance to.

"Shall we, then?" I asked.

Luisa nodded enthusiastically. "There's one more thing."

"What is it?"

"I don't want to talk to Dr. Benedict today."

Part of me wanted to suggest it would be good for her to talk to her therapist, but the wiser part of me accepted it was her decision. If she didn't believe speaking with the therapist would be helpful, then it wouldn't be. "You should do whatever feels right."

"My sister is pregnant."

"That's wonderful news! I'm happy for her and Ridge."

"You're probably wondering what my sister being pregnant has to do with Dr. Benedict."

I smiled, wanting so much to kiss her, but at the same time, wanting to hear whatever she had to say. "Now that you mention it…"

"I asked Seraphina why she hadn't said anything earlier. Her response was they wanted to keep it between the two of them for a while. Then she said, 'When the time comes you and the man you love find out you're having a baby together, I'm sure you'll feel the same way we did.' It's how I feel about you and me. I want to keep it between us for a while."

"Understood."

"It isn't that I want to hide it, either."

"I'm in complete agreement."

Luisa smiled. "I can't tell you how many times I've wondered if you're being honest when you say things like that."

"But now you know better."

"So, um, breakfast?"

"Good Lord, I completely forgot I offered to make it. You must be famished."

"We'll make it together."

I was astounded by the utter happiness I felt, particularly coming so soon after the devastation of losing my mother. I so wished she'd met Luisa. While I wasn't certain if I believed in an afterlife in the way most talked about it, a part of me felt as though my mum knew about her, knew she and I were together, had confessed our feelings for each other.

"What are you thinking about?" Luisa asked.

"My mother. You." I cupped her cheek with my palm. "I love you, Luisa. I've never said those words to anyone outside my family and certainly never in a romantic way. Please know the magnitude of the meaning behind my words."

"I do know, Press." Her eyes stayed riveted on mine. I laughed when she crossed them.

"What was that?"

"I'm *starving*."

I scooped her up in my arms and carried her into the kitchen.

"What are you doing?" she said, laughing the whole way.

"I like having you in my arms."

Luisa giggled but rested her head on my shoulder. "You mean so much to me, Press."

I deposited her on a stool near the kitchen counter. "I want to assure you I know the magnitude of the meaning behind your words." When I kissed her, she wrapped her arms around my neck and deepened it. I could've gone on kissing her for hours, but we both pulled away when we heard Beau and my father coming down the stairs.

I went around the counter to where I'd left half our breakfast ingredients.

"I'm driving your brother to the airport," my father said, motioning to the front door. "If you'd like to say goodbye," he added when I didn't react.

"Right. Of course." I stopped briefly when I reached Luisa.

"I'll wait here," she whispered. "Trust me when I say it's better if I do."

I followed my father into the foyer.

"You're off, then?" I said, not knowing what else to say.

"I don't know when I'll be back, Press."

"I understand, and I mean that."

He nodded and looked in the direction of the kitchen. "Tell Luisa I said goodbye."

"I will, Beau."

"Ready?" my father asked.

My brother and I embraced, but neither of us spoke. He was out the door and almost in the car when I hurried after him. "Beau? Wait."

He rested his arm on the open car door.

"I love you, Beau."

He half smiled. "I love you as well, Lavery."

I returned to the kitchen to find Luisa making much better progress than I had on breakfast.

"Sit down and relax," she said when I joined her.

"I can help."

She leaned up and kissed me. "Press, please let me take care you, for a change." It was the second time she'd said it. The first was the morning after my mother died. It wasn't easy for me to accept help or even care from others, but with her, I could.

"Thank you, Luisa."

After we'd finished our breakfast and I'd cleaned up while she relaxed, I asked her if she'd like to take a walk with me.

"Would you mind taking me to your mother's grave?" she asked.

"Not at all. If you'd like to visit it."

"Very much so."

We walked hand in hand, and when we arrived, Luisa held me as I cried. It was the comfort I'd yearned for on the day of the burial. "Thank you," I said again, wiping my tears. "I can't tell you what it means to me that you're here."

"It's where I want to be, Press. With you. Anywhere with you."

We spent the rest of the afternoon setting up "our" office in the veranda room, as Luisa called it. I reviewed several of the reports I required on a weekly basis and gave her access to the accounts I needed her to pull numbers from.

"We'll also set up a secure email."

Her eyes opened wide.

"What?" I asked, taking her hand in mine.

"I haven't checked mine. What if…"

"You have no need to worry." I took her hand and led her to the daybed, bringing my laptop with me. I opened a browser and did a search for her name. There were no results.

"I don't understand."

"All of your information has been eradicated both from the internet and the dark web. There are no means for the man who sent the message to find you again."

"I've just disappeared? Like I never existed?"

I searched my name and got the same results.

"You don't exist either?" she asked.

"The software, for lack of a better word, was developed by Laird Butler. It is used extensively in the intelligence world. As far as any email that is set up or your new phone, for example, all incoming and outgoing communication is being monitored. Not the communication itself, but where it's coming from or going to. You will not receive calls or messages from anyone who is not granted specific access."

"How did he find my number before?"

"I can't answer that, pet, but he won't be able to do it again. Ever."

"I want to do that thing, um, make a list of things we don't want to carry with us in the new year."

"Of course. Shall we do it now?"

Luisa nodded.

I pulled out several sheets of paper and tore them into smaller pieces. I handed half to her and kept half for myself. On the first sheet, I wrote, "The kiss." I held it out for her to see.

"You don't ever want to think about it again?"

"I do not."

She nodded a second time, picked up a few of the pieces I'd given her, and moved to the other side of the room, where she began to write. Out of the corner of my eye, I saw her fold each one several times.

"Now what?" she asked, motioning to a pile she'd made.

"We could burn them."

"I like that idea. All the bad stuff goes up in smoke."

"Precisely." I walked over to the fireplace, knelt down, and lit the wood that had been laid.

"I don't want to say them out loud," she said.

"You don't have to."

One by one, we tossed the paper into the fire.

"Good riddance," I said with the last of them.

"Good riddance," Luisa repeated.

28

Luisa

Press and I stayed in what we called the veranda room, and now our office, for the rest of the night. Earlier in the day, when he was reviewing the tasks I'd be helping with, I felt the same kind of excitement as I did when I started my MBA.

Only forty applicants were accepted into the graduate program, and rather than what might be considered traditional classes, we had meetings. Some were with the entire class, others were smaller and assignment-based.

During the first with all of us, I was stunned when the professor, who was the head of the program, said twenty-five percent of us in the room wouldn't make it to the end. Never, in a million years, did I dream I would be part of that statistic.

It was at Press' urging that I completed my degree, and now, I was so glad I had.

"Thank you," I said, raising my head to look up at him. We were seated on a sofa in front of the fireplace, wrapped in each other's arms.

"You're welcome," he said, kissing my forehead.

"Do you want to know what for?"

He smiled. "If you want to tell me."

"For suggesting I finish my degree. For giving me this opportunity to work with you."

"Barrett Family Enterprises will benefit greatly from having you on board. It's me who should be thanking you."

"Thanks for saying that."

He looked at his watch. "Almost time to begin the countdown."

"This is the best New Year's Eve I could imagine. In fact, if this is how we celebrate every year, I'd be happy."

Press leaned down and kissed me, and while I had no idea what time it was, that we stayed just like that, making out on the sofa like two teenagers for what felt like hours, had to mean it was what we were doing when the clock struck twelve.

The following morning, Press and I prepared a feast for the two of us and his father, who left shortly after we ate, saying he was off to spend the day with friends at another winery. I wondered where Beau spent New

Year's Eve. Something told me he'd been alone, and that saddened me.

"Stop biting your lip, pet," said Press, winking, then holding up his glass for a toast. "What's on your mind?" he asked after we each took a sip of mimosa.

"Wondering where Beau landed. Feeling sad he's probably alone."

Press nodded. "In years past, I would've predicted he'd be with a bevy of beauties. However, I think you're right that this is a very different year for him."

It hadn't been that long ago, yet it was hard for me to remember having feelings for him. Press was everything to me, whereas Beau was now an enigma.

He stroked the back of my hand with his thumb. "It was his choice to leave."

"I know, and I don't feel sorry for him. I'm thinking more about what you said about something missing from his life. I hope he finds it. I feel like I have." I leaned forward and kissed him.

"If someone told me I'd be sitting with you on New Year's Day, you kissing me, I never would've believed them."

"There isn't anywhere I'd rather be."

"What do you usually do on the first day of the new year?" he asked.

"I've spent almost every New Year's Eve and Day with Jada. Her family was always more fun than mine, so when she'd invite me over, I'd beg my mom to let me go." I looked at the phone Zeppelin gave me yesterday, hoping to see a message from her. "No one would've blocked her number, right?" I asked when there wasn't one.

"Definitely not. Why do you ask?"

"I sent her a message, but she hasn't responded."

"Perhaps she had a date."

"Do you know what the deal is between her and Zin?"

His eyes opened wide. "Zin? Do they even know each other?"

I told him about the odd exchange I'd witnessed between the two of them. "The weirdest part was the look on his face when I jokingly said she'd told me everything."

"While Zin and I certainly don't confide everything in each other, if he and Jada had any kind of, um, dalliance, I would certainly think he would've mentioned it." He shook his head and chuckled.

"What?" I asked.

"I was about to say he's much older than Jada. However, he's my age."

"And I'm Jada's age."

"Exactly."

"Zin seems older."

Press laughed out loud. "I was also about to say Jada seems younger."

The smile left my face. "She hasn't been through the same things I have."

Press stood and embraced me. "I'm sorry, pet. More than anything, I wish I could take the bad memories away."

I rested my cheek above his heart. "I wish you could too. That's what last night was for, though. I want to make room for joy this year."

"Precisely. Now, how shall we spend the rest of what I hope will be our first year together?"

My cheeks flushed when Press and I alone and naked in each other's arms flashed in my mind. I respected him when he said he wanted us to get to know each other better before we took another step in our relationship, but another part of me believed we should do what felt natural between us. Not wait because of some preconceived notion or jump into bed for the same reason.

Being with him, sharing kisses made it nearly impossible to tamp down my desire. Which didn't feel at all "natural."

Press put his fingertips on my chin and raised my face. "I'm feeling the same things you are, pet. I've never experienced the intensity of want, of yearning that I feel when I'm with you." He cleared his throat. "However, you should know this isn't new for me. Imagining you in the red bikini you wore poolside the day before the wedding, put me in a position of great potential embarrassment when we stood at the front of the chapel."

I giggled. "Really?"

He rested his forehead against mine. "Yes, really."

"I'm sorry to laugh, but you're always so... I don't know the right way to put it other than 'in control.'"

"You'd be surprised," he muttered, looking up at the ceiling. "When you're near, it's a constant struggle to keep how bad I want you in check."

"Then, why do you, Press?" Unable to resist, I unfastened the top button of his shirt and leaned forward to kiss the hollow of his neck.

When he groaned but tightened his grip on my shoulders rather than push me away, I unfastened another button.

"Luisa…"

"If you truly don't want this, you need to tell me," I murmured, releasing the third and fourth buttons and kissing the skin I'd just exposed. "Tell me," I repeated. "And I'll stop."

Rather than say a word, Press took a step back and held out his hand. I put mine in it, then led him to the staircase and up to the room where I first wished he'd get in bed with me rather than sit in a chair and read me a story.

Once there, I continued my plan to get him to finally let go of his steely control.

"Hands at your sides," I said, pulling his tucked-in shirt from his pants and unfastening his belt. I skimmed his taut abs with my fingers.

"Luisa," he hissed, clenching the fists he held rigidly at his sides.

How much more would it take, I wondered. When I knelt in front of him and began to lower the zipper of his trousers, I had my answer. Press roared out of his self-imposed bonds, lifting me not just to my feet, but into his arms. He carried me over to the bed. "I'll ask you the same, my darling. Are you certain this is what you want?"

"Want and need, Press." I watched as he tore his shirt from his body. "Let me see the rest of you first," I said, shaking my head when he reached out to remove my sweater. Never before had I been so bold. The truth was I didn't have a lot of experience with sex. I wasn't a virgin, but I couldn't say I'd ever had an orgasm. When Press dropped his trousers, freeing his rigid cock, I felt on the edge of my first.

I reached out and skimmed my fingers over it like I had his abs, and Press grabbed my wrist. "Let me," I demanded.

He hissed a second time when I wrapped my hand around him. "Like this, pet," he said through gritted teeth, putting his hand on top of mine and tightening my grip. I loved the feel of him, hard but velvety soft, so long and thick. When I leaned forward and touched him with the tip of my tongue, Press pulled away from me.

"I cannot wait another moment to be inside you, Luisa." His voice changed to a tone I'd never heard before from him—low and guttural. I pulled my sweater over my head and reached around to unfasten my bra. At the same time, Press lowered the zipper on my jeans and pulled them from my body.

It felt as though time stood still after the frantic pace with which we'd removed each other's clothes. Press stood where he was, barely moving, as he ran his gaze up and down my body.

"You are breathtaking," he murmured. "So beautiful, so exquisite."

"Press, please," I said, holding my hand out to him.

29

Press

I'd done more than let go; my passion, my desire, my want for Luisa left me feeling unhinged. I was a man possessed in his absolute need to have the woman I loved. The yearning I felt had been building for weeks, perhaps not from when I first laid eyes on her, but definitely from the first time I realized the complete trust and faith she put in me.

Had it been my only recourse, I would've accepted friendship alone from the woman who lay naked on my bed, her body visibly straining for my touch. Instead, I was about to make her mine. Forever. I couldn't accept anything less from her.

I settled my body between her spread legs, holding myself above her with both arms. I leaned in and pressed a kiss to one of her stiff nipples. When I sucked it into my mouth, the sensual sounds she made sent a bolt of lust straight through me.

After showering the same attention on her other breast, I slowly kissed my way down the center of her body, intermittently scattering kisses on her perfect porcelain skin like I'd longed to do every time I suffered through seeing her in that red bikini.

I shifted, resting my hands on the crease at the top of her thighs. I spread her folds open and softly blew on the bundle of nerves—the most sensitive place on her body—and watched as she shuddered and writhed.

"Press," she pleaded, her body jerking as I fluttered my tongue over her clit. I slid one finger into her wetness, and while I continued to ravish her with my tongue, I watched as her pleasure built. I licked down, delving deeper into her wetness, where soon, I would join our bodies together.

Luisa writhed and wove her fingers in my hair when I pressed my tongue against her clit.

"Press!" she shouted more than cried, tugging my hair. I held her hips still, swirled my tongue, and bent my finger inside her as she rode out her climax. Her eyes, tightly shut, eventually opened wide, and her gaze met mine. "Press," she repeated, the word sounding more like the purr of a kitten.

I shifted my body upward, using one arm to hold myself above her, and brought my mouth to hers. Her impassioned kiss dizzied me. My realization that I had no condoms left me feeling nearly bereft. I rolled to my side, still kissing her, stroking her hair.

"What's wrong?" she asked, her gaze so penetrating I felt we were connected through our eyes alone.

I cupped her cheek. "It is with the deepest regret I say I have no condoms, my darling."

Stunning me again, Luisa smiled.

"What?" I asked.

"I believe you're mistaken."

I pulled back and studied her, unable to keep my smile from matching hers. "If you're right, I would be the happiest man alive."

"So easily pleased," she teased, wriggling from my arms. She walked into the lavatory that separated my room from Beau's and returned with not just one condom, but a box.

"I was looking for a Q-tip earlier and stumbled upon these," she said, holding it out to me. "Oh, and I checked to make sure they haven't expired."

I took the box from Luisa's hand, set it behind me on the bed, pulled her into my arms, and continued kissing her as we'd been before.

"Happiest man alive," I repeated as I plucked one silver packet from the box, tore it open, and rolled it on.

"Happiest woman alive," Luisa said, pushing me onto my back. She straddled my hips and positioned my cock at her entrance. I put my hands on her waist, helping to slowly ease her onto me.

She was hot, wet, and so tight my eyes nearly rolled back in my head when I was finally buried as deep as I could go. I allowed Luisa to set her own pace, take her own pleasure, until my resolve finally snapped.

I rolled her under me, thrusting into her, pulling out slowly, then repeating the rhythm again and again. When I felt Luisa's body clenching mine, I brought my lips to hers, and we stared into each other's eyes. I had to feel connected to her in every way possible the first time she and I experienced the ultimate pleasure at the same time. I broke our kiss only long enough to roar my release and Luisa cried my name. When she raised her head and our lips met once again, I could feel the dampness of her tears.

"Luisa?"

She smiled but shook her head as more tears spilled onto her cheeks.

I brushed them with the pad of my thumb. "Tell me, did I hurt you, my darling?"

"No, Press. You didn't hurt me. It's the opposite. I never knew... I mean, I've never felt anything like that. It was...I don't think there's even a word for it."

"I can think of one, pet."

"Tell me."

"Love."

Luisa and I spent the rest of the day pleasuring one another's bodies and vowing to spend every New Year's Day just like this. When she said, "For the rest of our lives," my heart nearly burst with joy. I studied her, waiting for a sign she'd voiced more than she meant, but her eyes bored into mine as though she was waiting for me to challenge her or disagree.

I so wanted to hold her to it, ask her to be my wife, and ensure I'd spend every day with her, not just the first of the year. I resisted the urge to be so reckless, not because of insecurity, but because I knew it would completely overwhelm Luisa. This thing between us was days old—for her. She'd said she wasn't sure she knew how love felt. Once she did, then I'd propose. Luisa would never say the words unless she was certain she meant them. It was one of many things I admired about her.

The hardest thing, I found, was for me to take a step back and let her work through her feelings, especially her fear. I could assure her once an hour I'd keep her safe, but the fear that plagued her when she slept or when she got lost in thought and saw the signs of a panic attack coming on was something she had to process. No matter how many times she wrote a fear on a piece of paper and threw it into the fire, it wouldn't make any of it go away. Nor could I make it go away.

"What shall we do today?" I asked when we finally rolled out of bed on the second day of the year and made our way down to the kitchen.

"We should work," she responded emphatically.

"So anxious to start the daily grind?"

Luisa sipped her coffee. "Nervous," she responded.

I smiled but she didn't.

"Is there something I've done to give you pause?" I asked.

She walked over to the window and looked outside. "Not you."

I joined her and wrapped my arms around her waist. "There are just the two of us, my darling."

She turned and rested her hands on my shoulders. "Yesterday, when we were reviewing the work I'd be doing, I felt the same kind of excitement I had when I started my MBA, immediately followed by the same trepidation."

"What quelled your enthusiasm?"

"If you mean with my MBA, it was my first small-group project. There was one guy who was a total misogynist. It wasn't just me he disdained; it was all women. But, given I was the only female in our group, he singled me out. Either I wasn't making enough of a contribution or the work I did wasn't good enough for him. I came close to quitting the program because of him." Her cheeks flushed as if the admission embarrassed her. "My professor talked me into sticking it out, and I wound up with the best grade of the group. Of course, that only served to make the guy hate me even more."

"I'm proud of you for sticking it out."

She looked down at the floor. "I was bullied in high school because of my dad and the accident."

I cupped her cheek, and she looked up at me. "I wish I'd been there to protect you from it."

Luisa shrugged a shoulder. "I remember feeling the same way while I worked on that one project as I did back then—powerless against the bully."

"You said you received the highest mark among your fellow students, so you must've found the courage to overcome his treatment of you."

"I guess I did. However, feelings of inadequacy, of not being good enough, still plague me."

"I've said this before, but it can never be said enough. I have such admiration for you, Luisa—your strength, your tenacity, your drive, so many things about you." I smiled and leaned in to kiss her. "Perhaps especially the way you stand up to me."

"I feel safe with you, Press."

"There is no greater honor, my darling."

"I don't understand people who belittle others. I've never understood bigotry. Who is to say a man is better than a woman or a white person is better than a black person or an Asian person? Or a Christian better or worse than a Muslim."

"Prejudice of any kind is abhorrent. However, as I'm sure you know, hateful behavior stems more from the insecurity of the person spewing it than the person on the receiving end."

I was happy to see Luisa's smile finally return. "Kind of like, don't judge the behavior; look at the motivation behind it."

My cheeks flushed since I'd essentially just reiterated something she herself said. "Apologies. I learned that from you, didn't I?"

She shook her head. "I smiled because the first thing that came to mind was, you are going to be a wonderful father to our children, Press."

I blinked at the tears that flooded my eyes, hoping they wouldn't spill onto my cheeks. Alas, I was unsuccessful. "Do you really mean that?" I whispered more than said as I brushed the dampness on my cheeks away with the back of my hand.

Luisa put her arms around me. "With all my heart."

"I don't think anyone has ever said anything that means more to me, my darling."

"I mean it, Press. Not just that you'll be an amazing dad, but if I close my eyes, I can see you and me raising our kids together."

I put my hand on my heart and chuckled. "Who knew I was such a weeper?"

"You love so well, Press. Me especially. Your father is the same with you and Beau, and I have no doubt your mother is equally responsible, if not more so."

"Okay, my love, you have now reduced me to an emotional wreck."

Luisa leaned forward and kissed me. "If I was only allowed one wish for the year ahead, it would be that you'd let your guard down, lower your walls, lose your inhibitions"—she winked—"with me. Now, would you like to take a walk first or get right to work?"

30

Luisa

Press and I took a lovely stroll through the vine-yards before we settled at our makeshift desks and got to work.

"What's on your mind, pet," he asked partway through our day.

"I still haven't heard from Jada." I'd been looking down at my phone, but when I looked up, Press was studying me.

"Would you like me to check with Zin?"

"Would it be weird if you did?" I asked.

"I don't believe so," he responded, winking.

"It just isn't like her. You said you were sure she has the number, right?"

"I'm certain. Also, your message to her was marked delivered, was it not?"

I checked my phone, and he was right. Not that it made me feel any better.

"Zin is seeing if she's at home," he said.

Press' phone buzzed, and I looked up. "What's wrong?" I asked.

"There seems to be some confusion. Apparently, Mrs. Yáñez thinks Jada is still at Butler Ranch."

"That makes no sense. She went home three days ago."

Press' phone buzzed again but, this time, with a call. "It's Zin."

"Go ahead," I said, motioning for him to answer.

"Luisa is here with me," he stated before anything else.

"Hey, Luisa," Zin said when Press propped the phone on the counter so we could both see him.

"Hi." I gave him a quick wave.

Zin hung his head, then scrubbed his face. "Okay, so here's the deal. When Jada left Butler Ranch the other night, she didn't go straight home."

"You left right after she did," I mumbled, remembering that I'd watched him drive off.

"That's right."

"Where did you both go?" Press asked.

"My place. She was there when I arrived. She stayed until yesterday afternoon, which is why Mrs. Yáñez thought she was still at Butler Ranch. The only problem is, like I said, she left *yesterday* afternoon. I thought she was going home."

"You *thought* she was going home?"

I put my hand on Press' arm. He was agitated. However, Zin and Jada were adults in the same way we were. Them spending a couple of nights together wasn't the issue. What worried me to the point where I felt a panic attack coming on was that she still wasn't home.

"Where is she?" Press asked him.

"I was hoping you could tell me."

I looked up and saw Jaicon, Magnet, and Tank were headed in our direction.

Press followed my line of sight. "Where are you now?"

"Still at my place."

"I'll ring you back."

Press ended the call and met the group at the front door. "Jada Yáñez is missing," he said, waving them inside before they had a chance to speak.

"We intercepted something," said Jaicon, looking from me to Press.

"What?" I asked.

"Another message."

I felt dizzy and grabbed Press' arm.

"Give us a minute," he said, leading me into a living room I hadn't been in before and over to a sofa. "Tell me how you want to handle this, Luisa."

I knew what he was asking. Did I want to know what the message was, or did I want him to shield me from it? I gripped both his hands with mine. The idea that I'd be in here alone while he read it, scared me. Knowing what the message was, terrified me. "I don't know."

"Press?" said Jaicon from behind me. "This is urgent."

He studied me, and I nodded.

"You're certain?" he asked.

"I can do this as long as you're with me."

"Come in," he said, motioning to her.

"It was sent from Ms. Yáñez's phone," she began.

"Is she alive?" I whispered.

Jaicon's eyes met mine. "She is."

"He has her, doesn't he?"

She nodded.

"My God," I heard Press say under his breath.

I put my hand in front of my mouth to stifle the sound that came from somewhere deep in my chest. I could not lose it. *Couldn't.* That Jaicon was here meant this involved me somehow. "Tell me," I said, squaring my shoulders and tightening my grip on Press' hands.

She sat down on the other side of me. "This message came in the form of a video. It is of a woman we believe is Ms. Yáñez. She has been tortured."

As sick as I felt, I knew I had to hear the rest.

"The person who sent it has very specific instructions. He will free Ms. Yáñez—"

"Her name is Jada," I said.

"He will free Jada in exchange for Luisa. He has explicit instructions."

"No fucking way," Press seethed. His eyes conveyed the same panic I felt but knew I had to tamp down.

"What are the instructions?" I asked.

Jaicon looked at Press, who was still shaking his head.

"What are they?" I shouted.

"He wants you to come to where he's holding her. He said if he sees or hears anyone other than you, he'll kill her."

"Where is he holding her?"

"Once he receives a response to his message, he'll tell you where to go."

"This is ludicrous," Press muttered.

"I want to see it."

"No. Absolutely not," he said, shaking his head more violently than he had been.

"Press." I waited until his eyes met mine. "I have to see it."

"*I'll* watch it."

"No. I have to do this."

He shook his head again. "No, Luisa."

"Listen to me. I have to see it," I repeated. "I want you with me when I do, but—"

"I will not leave you alone. Not for a single second."

"Jaicon?"

This time, she didn't look at Press. Her eyes stayed on mine when she called out to Magnet.

The man came around and placed a tablet on the table. "The voice has been digitally enhanced to make it unrecognizable, and the only person visible is Jada."

I nodded and took a deep breath. "Go ahead."

The video appeared on the screen. In it, Jada was tied to a wall in the same way the woman in the photo sent with the previous message had been. The hardest part was I could hear Jada's whimpers.

"Luisa, my Luisa," the voice began. "I told you, next time, you won't escape before we've had our fun. Sadly, your best friend beat you to it." The voice cackled. "She begged so prettily for me to let her go that I finally agreed to her suggestion. When she said, 'Trade me for her,' I had to admit it was a brilliant solution." There were more cackles. "Here is how it will go. When you arrive, I will be standing with the barrel of my gun resting against your best friend's temple. If I hear any voice or see any face other than yours, she will die instantly. Reply to this message with the words 'I'm yours' to receive your next set of instructions." The screen went black.

"Zeppelin is working with our friends at NRO to triangulate the location using cell towers. Once we've done that, we'll use overheads to get a clear read on where Jada is being held."

I shook my head. "Don't bother. I know where she is."

"Where?" asked Press.

I motioned for Magnet to replay the video. When it popped up on the screen, I pointed to the upper right corner. "See that? It's an on-air sign."

"Like for a radio or TV show?" Tank asked.

"Yes." I pointed to it again. "Look at the lower left corner. Part of it is cracked, and someone tried to fix it with blue adhesive."

Magnet zoomed in on it. "Yeah?"

"That's at KCRP, SLO CAL's underground radio station. Most believe it's off campus, but it isn't. It's housed beneath the oldest building. Jada and I did an internship there when we were in high school."

"Zin worked for the radio station during undergrad," said Press.

"That's right. He was there when we were. Not that we ever saw him."

Tank and Jaicon both placed calls at the same time a helicopter, bigger than the one we'd flown here in, landed just outside the window of the room where we were seated.

"Zin—I need to call him back," said Press.

Jaicon nodded when he looked over at her.

"Vaile, there is no easy way to say this," he began. I listened as he relayed what was in the message—everything other than where Jada was being held. I could hear his cry of anguish through the phone.

"Where the fuck does this sonuvabitch have her?"

"You'll receive updates as we know more," Press responded before ending the call.

"You did the right thing by not telling him," I said when Press covered his eyes with his hand.

"If it were me, I'd never forgive him for it."

"He'd get her killed."

Press nodded and looked up when Tank approached.

"NRO just confirmed the same location," he reported. "Let's move out."

"Wait!" I shouted when he, Jaicon, and Magnet ran in the direction of the French doors that led out to the lawn. "I'm going too."

My eyes met Press'. I expected him to argue, tell me no, even try to stop me from leaving, but he did none of those things. "You heard the man; let's move out." He stood and held his hand out to me before turning to Jaicon and mouthing two words. *"Los Caballeros."*

She nodded once.

"Is that an Akicita?" Press shouted as we ran out behind Tank.

"Sure as hell is. We'll land in *SLO CAL* in under an hour," said Zeppelin, who arrived with Atticus and Blackjack just as we were climbing inside.

31

Press

The Akicita helicopter we were in was one of, if not the fastest in the world. It was also big enough to carry twelve passengers along with tactical gear—which I was being outfitted in.

There was a time in my life when experiencing a night like this would've been my fondest dream. Instead, it was a horrible nightmare.

My instincts screamed at me to protect the woman I loved at any cost. Yet, there was a voice in my head yelling equally as loud, telling me if I didn't follow her lead, do this with her, I'd lose her forever because she'd never forgive me.

"Your team is deploying," Jaicon said through the comms.

"Copy that," I responded.

Our "secret" brotherhood had existed for hundreds of years, through many generations, but had it truly ever been as secret as we'd assumed? Was anything truly secret? And what kind of games had we been playing all that time? Believing we were vigilantes, thinking we could help those who needed it? It had been a blanket statement, but looking back, if we hadn't been smart enough to ask for assistance from K19, I may have never known Luisa. She may still be in the hands of the lunatic who now held Jada.

I studied the group of people flying with us. If I had to guess, each of them—including the Brits—was either former or current NRO themselves or with the CIA's Special Activities Division. Regardless of whether I was right or wrong, I had every confidence Jada Yáñez would be rescued within minutes of our arrival.

I also had no doubt they knew more about Los Caballeros than I did.

The person I was most worried about, besides Luisa and Jada, was Zin. The worry he'd act without any thought to his own safety, while causing more risk to Jada's life once he learned where she was being held captive, was the reason I'd asked Jaicon to bring in the rest of the *caballeros*.

While I hadn't divulged where she was, I had to tell him what was in the video. Like Luisa would never forgive me if I'd tried to stop her from getting in this helicopter, Zin would see it as a betrayal if he learned

I had knowledge of her abduction and hadn't told him. Our friendship would be over. It still might be if he found out I'd had the information he sought when he asked where she was, and hadn't told him.

I looked over at Luisa, who was currently head-to-head with Jaicon and Zeppelin, viewing a three-dimensional schematic of the building where the radio station was—focusing primarily on the basement.

Atticus, seated beside me, was compiling a list of everyone who'd worked there since its inception.

"Can you take a look at this list?" he asked, moving closer to Luisa.

I watched as she studied it for a few seconds, then gasped.

"Which one?" Atticus asked.

She pointed, then looked up at me.

"Who is he?" I asked.

"The fucking misogynist from my program."

The one she said held disdain for all women but that something about her seemed to bother him even more. I took a closer look at the name she'd pointed to. *Hamad Al Zaabi.*

Within seconds, Atticus had a dossier loaded.

"That's him," confirmed Luisa when he pointed to a photograph.

"NRO says they can place him in Egypt four days ago," said Magnet from the other side of the helicopter.

Like in Felixstowe, I sat in awe as the team mapped out the plan to rescue Jada while, at the same time, capturing the man who held her hostage.

"We *need* him alive," Jaicon repeated more than once. "The Akicita will land here," she said, pointing to the tablet, where an image of the area surrounding the outside of the building appeared.

"The K19 team already at the location has confirmed Al Zaabi has eyes and ears throughout the corridors," Zeppelin reported.

"What does that mean?" Luisa asked.

"Nothing we hadn't anticipated," Jaicon responded. "It's how he's ensuring no one enters instead of you or with you."

The thoughts racing through my mind dizzied me, and I put my head in my hands. "Are you actually suggesting that she go in *alone*?"

I felt Luisa's eyes on me, but I couldn't look at her. It was one thing for her to insist she be here. It was another thing entirely for her to be unprotected, at the mercy of a madman.

"Luisa will not go in alone." Jaicon pulled up the schematic. "We will have eyes on her when she enters through this corridor—"

"How is that not alone?"

I felt Luisa's hand on my arm. "Press, let her finish."

"May I?" Zeppelin asked.

Jaicon nodded, handed him the tablet, and motioned for me to switch places with her.

Zeppelin dragged his finger where the other corridors were indicated. As he did, each was highlighted.

"Doc Butler and his father are working with the team now to intercept the signals within these areas. Al Zaabi will not be aware the transmissions he's hearing and seeing have been tampered with in any way. The feeds will be replaced. The only section that will remain hot is the one where Luisa will enter from. By the time we land, we'll have a full live view of the station's interior. If he takes a step or even lifts a finger, we'll know it."

"Nothing you've said changes the fact Luisa will be going in alone."

Zeppelin ran his finger along both sides of the corridor she'd enter through, then shaded parts of the area. "Signals from everywhere shaded will be intercepted. We will be there, but Al Zaabi won't know it."

"Wait, is that above where she'll be?" I asked.

The schematic on the screen rotated. "These are drop ceilings with a minimum of three feet of crawl space throughout. The walls"—he pointed—"are cinder block and twenty-four-inches thick, allowing us ample support."

"What if he hears you?" Luisa asked, rubbing her temples with her fingers.

"By the time you enter the building, snipers will already be in place. The minute there is any chance he can be neutralized, he will be."

"Meaning if he does hear you and wants to shoot Jada, you'll be able to shoot him first? How?"

Jaicon put her hand on Luisa's arm. "You need to trust us."

Luisa shook her head, and Jaicon looked up at Zeppelin.

"This is the only option," he said. "Either we're with you, or you don't go in at all."

Luisa's eyes met mine, but neither of us spoke.

"Before we go any further, I need you to confirm if you're in or out."

"In," Luisa responded, turning away from me to look Jaicon in the eye.

"You're certain?"

"Absolutely."

Jaicon nodded, and Zeppelin handed the tablet back to her. "The team will rendezvous here." She pointed at a location several yards from the building.

She tapped the screen, and multiple shapes appeared along with one X, which she indicated first. "That's Luisa's entry point." Then, she pointed to each circle. "These are where snipers will be positioned. Additional backup is indicated by each of the squares."

"Meaning?" I asked.

"K19."

"What will Los Caballeros be doing?"

"Assisting in monitoring the action within the station itself as well as in the corridors."

"Will Zin be part of that team?" I asked.

"Negative," Jaicon responded. When she didn't say anything further, I figured there must be a reason why not. As much as I wanted to ask, I held back.

"Where will I be?"

"Here, with me," Jaicon pointed to an area no more than five feet from where a corridor intercepted the one Luisa would be in. "If we're forced to abort for any reason, you get Luisa, by any means necessary, and retrace our entry route. Tank will be waiting."

Right before the helicopter began its descent, Jaicon sent the reply to Al Zaabi via Luisa's phone.

The response was immediate. In it, he reminded Luisa what would happen to Jada if she did not arrive alone. She was given exactly thirty minutes from the time of his response to arrive at the radio station, which he identified by its call letters. If she did not, Jada would die.

As soon as the helicopter touched down, the team exited and moved out to the rendezvous point in the same choreographed manner I'd witnessed in Felixstowe. We were within steps of the others when I put my hand on Luisa's arm.

"Are you absolutely certain about this?" I asked again.

"Jada will not die because of my cowardice."

We waited as each of the operatives reported via comms when they were in position. Once they all were, Jaicon signaled me to activate the NVG and camera built into the Ops-Core helmet I wore, then motioned for us to follow her into the building's underground labyrinth. We'd reached the lower level and were about to separate when gunfire erupted.

"Abort, abort!" came through the comms.

"No!" cried Luisa, racing toward the station's door. Jaicon's words echoed in my head, "…any means necessary." I grabbed her around the waist and hoisted her over my shoulder, then ran in the opposite direction, retracing our steps. As we rounded the first corner, Tank met us.

"You got her?"

"Negative," I responded, panting. As much as my pride wanted the adrenaline coursing through my bloodstream to be enough for me to carry her the rest of the way, I was not trained for this. Particularly since the woman I held in my arms was doing her level best to get me to drop her while causing me as much bodily injury as she could.

At the same time Tank grabbed her, my comms went dead. I could no longer hear what was happening inside the station or any instructions I may be issued.

"What happened?" I shouted once we reached the door leading outside and were met by Tryst and Brix.

"The motherfucker shot him!" Tank shouted back.

He set Luisa on her feet and reentered the building without saying anything more. Knowing she would attempt to follow, I grabbed her around the waist and held her to me.

"Let them do their job. *Please, Luisa.*"

She nodded.

"Over here," said Ridge, motioning us to a waiting SUV.

"Who was shot?" I asked once we were inside and had removed our ballistic helmets.

"Al Zaabi."

"By whom?"

"Zin."

"What about Jada?" Luisa demanded.

"I don't know," Ridge responded. My eyes met his in the rearview mirror, and in them, I saw the same worry I felt. "The comms system and the monitors went down as soon as the gunfire erupted and we heard the command to abort," he added.

My own hadn't ceased operation until several seconds later.

I raised my head when the door of the building Luisa and I had exited reopened. Two men raced out. One, who I knew was Zin, carried someone wrapped in a blanket in his arms.

"Who is that with him?" I asked, pointing to the other man.

"Onyx," Ridge responded.

My eyes opened wide. While I should have expected Jada's brother to be part of the K19 team, I hadn't. It was my understanding he was currently residing on the East Coast.

"Let me out, dammit!" Luisa cried, trying to open the passenger door as we watched the two men run to the waiting Akicita.

"That's Doc," said Ridge, pointing as the third man got in the helicopter. As soon as he was inside, it lifted off.

The front passenger door opened, and Brix got in. "Jada is alive. They're transporting her to Summerdale Community Medical Center."

"What are you waiting for? *Go!*" Luisa shouted.

It took under five minutes to drive the two and a half kilometers to the medical center where Brix had said Jada was being transported.

"Is there another heliport?" I asked when we arrived, pointing to the one that sat empty.

"Not that I'm aware of," Brix replied, looking over the seat at me with scrunched eyes, then back at his mobile. "This says Summerdale," he confirmed. "There's no other hospital on the Central Coast with the same name." He typed something on the phone's screen. "Correction. No other hospital with that name in the State of California."

When Ridge pulled up to the emergency-room entrance, Brix exited the vehicle and ran inside. He returned within minutes. "The helicopter never arrived nor was it expected."

"Where is she?" Luisa cried, the fight seemingly leaving her.

32

Press

"I don't know, pet, but Tryst says we're to meet at Butler Ranch," I said, reading the message I'd received on my mobile.

The four of us were mostly silent on the half-hour drive, but the tension was so thick it felt palpable. While I was relieved beyond measure that Luisa was safe and the man we believed was behind the bounty for her was dead, there were still so many unknowns. He couldn't have acted alone, and even though Varilla said he knew she'd been targeted specifically but not by whom, I didn't believe him.

Worse in immediacy was where Jada had been taken and determining the severity of her condition. There was a chance that a decision had been made en route to transport her to a different medical center. Once we reached Butler Ranch, I prayed, as much for Luisa's sake as my own, there would be an update.

"Did you know Onyx was in town?" Ridge asked Brix.

"Yeah. He and his wife flew in to spend the holidays with his mom and siblings. They're staying with my mom."

Onyx and his siblings were Brix's cousins, which meant he had to be equally torn up about Jada. I reached over the seat and squeezed his shoulder. He put his hand on mine. "Thanks, man."

After Ridge pulled through the gate of the ranch and we crested the hill, I was stunned to see the Akicita.

"They brought her here?" Luisa gasped. "Why would they do that?"

I put my hand on hers. "We'll soon find out."

"Doc is a physician's assistant. He wouldn't have allowed it if it wasn't safe to do so," said Brix.

Luisa turned to me. "You *saw* the video."

"Dalton is here," said Ridge, pointing to a vehicle when he pulled up in front of the main house.

"Was he in Felixstowe?" she asked.

"He was responsible for the entire triage."

"That makes me feel a little better."

I nodded. I'd witnessed the organized and disciplined way the man we called Bones navigated and oversaw the medical treatment for over five hundred victims. As Brix had said about Doc, if Ridge's brother believed it was unsafe for Jada to be here rather than in a hospital, she wouldn't be.

I got out of the SUV when Ridge parked, and walked around to open Luisa's door. Rather than get out, she remained seated, looking off in the distance.

"Luisa?"

She shook her head, and tears ran down her cheeks. "What happened to her is my fault."

"The fault lies solely with the man who abducted her, my darling."

"He wanted *me*. I don't know if I can face her."

"She needs you, Luisa," I heard a voice say from behind me. I spun around and embraced Zin.

"How is she?" I asked.

"Her injuries aren't life-threatening. Bones said she wasn't drugged." He looked away, and like Luisa, his eyes filled with tears. "But she's catatonic."

When I heard Luisa's anguished cry, I spun back around and gathered her in my arms. I held her as she clung to me and sobbed. Tears ran down my own cheeks, and I had no doubt Zin was crying equally as hard.

I looked up at the porch when I saw someone come outside. Sorcha and Laird stood with their arms around each other.

"What about Esmeralda?" I asked.

"Onyx is with Jada now and will ask his siblings to meet him at his mother's house soon. He wants to tell her as well as his brothers and sisters what happened in person," said Zin.

The front door of the main house opened again, and Ridge came out with Seraphina and Leah. Both women ran over to us. Luisa let go of me, and I helped her out of the SUV before taking a step back. While they embraced, I put my arm around Zin's shoulders.

"I don't know what to say."

He shook his head. "You knew where she was."

"I did, and I'm sorry I didn't tell you."

"I understand why you didn't."

"You do?

"I might've gotten her killed." He looked over at Luisa, her sister, and mother. "I almost did anyway," he said under his breath.

"While I don't know exactly what went down, I do know you saved her life, my friend. So, who did tell you?"

"Doc. It was better that way." His shoulders slouched forward, and his tears continued. "I should get back inside."

"Go ahead. We'll be in shortly."

He nodded. "Jada needs her," he said, motioning to Luisa.

"Understood."

I followed as the women walked arm in arm toward the house. When they reached the porch steps, Luisa let go and turned around.

"I need you with me, Press."

"Of course." I took her hand, and we walked up to the front door. Sorcha and Laird had gone back inside. I put my hand on the doorknob, but Luisa hesitated. "You can do this, pet," I said, squeezing her hand. "I'll be right beside you."

She nodded, and we went inside, where Doc was waiting.

"Before I take you back, I want you to know what to expect." He motioned us to the sofa. The three of us sat, Luisa between him and me. "Zin said he told you Jada hasn't spoken."

"He did," I responded when Luisa didn't.

"Dalton started an IV, administered pain medication, then conducted a thorough examination. The wounds on Jada's back were caused by a cat o' nine tails. There are some lacerations. However, the majority of them are not deep. The implement Al Zaabi used is more consistent with what's known as BDSM impact play. While it is not designed the same way as the weapon used historically to inflict severe physical punishment, repeated thrashings on the same area can result in the lacerations I mentioned. Some of them required stitches, but not all. Our main concern now is preventing infection."

The longer Doc spoke, the tighter Luisa gripped my hand. I watched as she listened, wishing Doc hadn't gone into as much detail as he did, but accepting she needed to know before she saw her friend.

"You mentioned Dalton administered pain medication. Is Jada awake presently?" I asked.

"She was when I came out. However, I would anticipate her going in and out of sleep."

I squeezed Luisa's hand rather than ask if she was ready to see her. She nodded, and we stood, following Doc.

He stopped at the door and turned to her.

"I'm ready," she said.

Zin was sitting on the far side of the bed, stroking Jada's hair. Bones, who'd been standing beside Zin, walked around us. "I'll be right outside," he said.

Luisa grabbed his hand, and he stopped.

"Thank you," she whispered.

He gave her a head nod and left the room.

"Sweetheart, Luisa is here," Zin whispered.

My eyes met his when Jada's eyes opened and she reached for Luisa's hand.

"Leave us," Jada whispered when she sat in the chair at the side of her bed.

"Go ahead," Luisa said, looking at Zin, then over her shoulder at me.

Zin stood, leaned down, and kissed Jada's forehead the same way I did so often with Luisa. We stepped out and closed the door behind us. Bones, as promised, was waiting right outside.

"She asked us to leave them alone," said Zin, smiling.

"Who did?" Bones asked.

"Jada."

Bones leaned against the wall and sighed. "That's a good sign."

"It's the first she's spoken a single word," said Zin, turning to me. "She held out her hand."

"That's good too," said Bones. "If it's okay with you guys, I'm going to take a quick break. I'll be close by, so if I'm needed, just holler."

"Will do," said Zin, leaning against the wall like Bones had. "You're probably wondering why I never said anything about Jada and me."

"I'm not."

His eyes met mine, and I saw another ghost of a smile. "I don't believe you."

"Luisa said something to me a couple of days ago. It was actually something Seraphina said to her. This is not verbatim, but when you love someone, sometimes the two of you want to keep it just between yourselves for a while."

"I do love her, Press."

"I know you do," I said, squeezing his shoulder. "It's evident."

He looked beyond me in the direction of the main rooms of the house, then leaned closer. "I killed the motherfucker," he said, hardly above a whisper.

"Tank said something to that effect."

"I know they wanted him alive, but I just"—he shook his head—"*couldn't*. Ya know?"

"I do know. I would've done the very same thing."

"Varilla needs to die too. He knew. I'd bet my own life on it."

"I'll admit I had the same thought."

"It's in Ares' hands now," he said, his voice still low. "But if that *sonuvabitch* is ever let out of prison, I'll hunt him down and torture him far worse than Jada was. Then I'll kill him."

"We'll do it together."

I hadn't kept track of how much time Zin and I remained in the hallway, leaning against the wall, neither of us speaking again. I stood up straight when the door opened just slightly.

"She's asking for you," Luisa said, stepping aside to let Zin enter. She came out and closed the door behind her.

I opened my arms, and we embraced, her tears dampening my shirt.

"She wanted me to know she didn't tell him to exchange me for her." Luisa shook her head. "It was so important to her to say it, even though I told her I knew she hadn't." She bit her lip. "She wouldn't talk about it otherwise."

"That's to be expected. Zin said she hadn't spoken at all prior to your arrival."

"How is she?" asked Bones, rejoining us.

"I'm not sure how to answer that other than to say Zin is with her now. She asked for him," Luisa told him.

"I'll check on them in a little while," he said, returning to the main rooms.

Luisa took my hand, and we followed. Instead of joining those gathered in the living room, she led me outside and over to the porch swing we'd sat in so many times when she first came to stay with Laird and Sorcha.

"She's going to be okay," Luisa said. "Like for me, her recovery won't be easy. In some ways, what she went through was harder; in some ways, it wasn't."

I cupped her cheek with my palm and stared into her eyes. "I am so proud of you, Luisa. More, I'm in awe of you. Your strength, the way you've worked so hard to heal." My voice was clogged with emotion, and I couldn't continue.

"I couldn't have done any of it without you, Press."

I smiled. "Yes, you would've."

She shook her head. "You're wrong, but I don't want us to argue. There's something I need to tell you." Luisa gripped both my hands in hers and turned her body so she was facing me. "I love you, Lavery Barrett. I know I said I wasn't sure how love felt, but I am now. I love you so much."

"And I, you, pet."

We sat in each other's arms, love flowing between us. The last several weeks had been filled with utter devastation and unimaginable loss. If there had been another way for Luisa and me to meet, to get to know one another, to fall in love, I'd trade it in a heartbeat. But here we were, the two of us together, rising from the ashes like a phoenix.

"I had a thought about Jada," Luisa said, raising her head from my shoulder.

"What's that?"

"Do you think Tryst would let her and Zin stay at *El Lugar de Curación?*"

"I am certain of it."

Epilogue

Luisa

In the same way I'd been the one to initiate it when Press and I first made love, I was the one who proposed.

We'd returned to Napa after spending the remainder of the week at Seahorse. Two nights later, I insisted on making dinner while he relaxed, then asked him to join me at the dining table. In my hands, I carried a plate covered by a silver dome. Once he was seated, I placed it in front of him.

"Go ahead," I said, when he looked at me with scrunched eyes. He removed the dome and picked up the card that rested on the plate.

"Please join Lavery Barrett and Luisa Reeve, February 14, as they become man and wife, partners in the vast and wondrous universe," he read out loud.

"Will you marry me, Press?" I asked.

"To do so will make me the happiest man alive."

"And me, the happiest woman."

He stood and we kissed.

"What do you say we go use more of those condoms?" I said.

"What about dinner?"

I raised a brow.

"Right."

"I love you, Press."

"I love you more, Luisa."

Keep reading for a sneak peek
at the next book in the
Wicked Winemakers Central Coast
First Label series,

Zin's Sin

He kept his emotions locked away.
She made him her secret escape.
Together, can they build a relationship that
survives beyond the shadows?

ZIN

I've cultivated a reputation as the city's notorious play-boy, until Jada Yáñez shattered all my defenses. When she was kidnapped, I risked everything to find her. Now that she's safe, I want more than our secret nights together. But with her trauma still fresh, I fear she'll see my desire for commitment as pity rather than love.

JADA

My kidnapping left scars deeper than the physical ones. I never expected Zin—my passionate, secret lover—would become my protector. As nightmares continue to haunt me, I find strength in his devotion. But can I trust that his sudden desire for more comes from love and not from seeing me as broken?

1

Zin

"Hi," I said, brushing hair from the forehead of the woman I'd taken another's life in order to save.

She flinched and moved away as though my touch scorched her flesh. Almost worse, her eyes wouldn't meet mine.

"Jada?"

"Don't touch me."

They were the first words she'd spoken directly to me since I held her in my arms and carried her out of the place where a madman had strung her up against a wall and proceeded to repeatedly whip and torture her for God knew how long.

"I don't want you here."

I landed in the chair as much as sat. "I don't understand."

"You need to leave, Zin."

"But…Luisa said you asked me to come in."

"To tell you to go. Leave."

"Jada…Jesus, would you look at me?"

"Go, Zin."

"Tell me why."

She took a deep breath. "I don't need a reason."

"What did I—"

"Get out!" she shouted, her eyes meeting mine for the first time.

"What the fuck did I do, besides save your life?"

"If it weren't for you, I never would've been in danger in the first place."

About the Author

USA Today best-selling author Heather Slade writes shamelessly sexy, edge-of-your seat romantic suspense.

She gave herself the gift of writing a book for her own birthday one year. Sixty-plus books later (and counting), she's having the time of her life.

The women Slade writes are self-confident, strong, with wills of their own, and hearts as big as the Colorado sky. The men are sublimely sexy, seductive alphas who rise to the challenge of capturing the sweet soul of a woman whose heart they'll hold in the palm of their hand forever. Add in a couple of neck-snapping twists and turns, a page-turning mystery, and a swoon-worthy HEA, and you'll be holding one of her books in your hands.

She loves to hear from her readers. You can contact her at heather@heatherslade.com

To keep up with her latest news and releases, please visit her website at www.heatherslade.com to sign up for her newsletter.

MORE FROM AUTHOR HEATHER SLADE

ROMANTIC SUSPENSE

K19 SECURITY
SOLUTIONS
TEAM ONE
Razor's Edge
Gunner's Redemption
Mistletoe's Magic
Mantis' Desire
Dutch's Salvation

K19 SECURITY
SOLUTIONS
TEAM TWO
Striker's Choice
Monk's Fire
Halo's Oath
Tackle's Honor
Onyx's Awakening

K19 SHADOW
OPERATIONS
TEAM ONE
Code Name: Ranger
Code Name: Diesel
Code Name: Wasp
Code Name: Cowboy
Code Name: Mayhem

K19 ALLIED
INTELLIGENCE
TEAM ONE
Code Name: Ares
Code Name: Cayman
Code Name: Poseidon
Code Name: Zeppelin
Code Name: Magnet

K19 ALLIED
INTELLIGENCE
TEAM TWO
Code Name: Puck
Code Name:
Michelangelo
Code Name: Typhon
Code Name: Hornet
Code Name: Reaper

K19 GENESIS
CONSORTIUM
TEAM ONE
Blackjack's Ascent
Dagger's Shield
Sundance's Trail
Nomad's Compass
Preacher's Decree

K19 SENTINEL
CYBER
TEAM ONE
Code Name: Admiral
Code Name: Dante
Code Name: Grit
Code Name: Tank
Code Name: Atticus

K19 SENTINEL
CYBER
TEAM TWO
Code Name: Kodiak
Code Name: Paragon
Code Name: Vex
Code Name: Shredder
Code Name: Jagger

PROTECTORS
UNDERCOVER
TEAM ONE
Undercover Agent
Undercover Emissary
Undercover Savior
Undercover Infidel
Undercover Shadow

ROYAL AGENTS
OF MI6
Make Me Shiver
Drive Me Wilder
Feel My Pinch
Chase My Shadow
Find My Angel

THE INVINCIBLES
TEAM ONE
Code Name: Deck
Code Name: Edge
Code Name: Grinder
Code Name: Rile
Code Name: Smoke

THE INVINCIBLES
TEAM TWO
Code Name: Buck
Code Name: Irish
Code Name: Saint
Code Name: Hammer
Code Name: Rip

THE
UNSTOPPABLES
TEAM ONE
Code Name: Fury
Code Name: Merried

MORE FROM AUTHOR HEATHER SLADE